The Public Eye

A PORT CITY HIGH NOVEL

SHANNON FREEMAN

SADDLEBACK
PUBLISHING

High School High

Taken

Deported

The Public Eye

Copyright ©2014 by Saddleback Educational Publishing
All rights reserved. No part of this book may be reproduced in any form or by any means, electronic or mechanical, including photocopying, recording, scanning, or by any information storage and retrieval system, without the written permission of the publisher. SADDLEBACK EDUCATIONAL PUBLISHING and any associated logos are trademarks and/or registered trademarks of Saddleback Educational Publishing.

ISBN-13: 978-1-62250-040-6
ISBN-10: 1-62250-040-7
eBook: 978-1-61247-683-4

Printed in Guangzhou, China
NOR/1113/CA21302125

18 17 16 15 14   1 2 3 4 5

ACKNOWLEDGMENTS

I feel that I need to thank my family for being so supportive. Whether you are purchasing books or showing up to book signings, it is appreciated. Being one of the youngest in my family, I have always felt your support and love no matter where my heart's desires have taken me. A special thanks to the Warrick family, Ford family, Freeman family, Francis family, Loivolette family, and Woods family. I have a small piece of each one of you in me.

Arianne McHugh, you changed my life. Thank you so much for having an open mind and helping me navigate through this new world. You are an awesome tour guide. I hope I live up to all of your expectations. I know that you went out on a limb for me. I am forever indebted to you.

Thank you to everyone who has read any of my books and taken the time to write me and let me know how much you enjoyed it. Your words of encouragement have been so touching. I'm still so new to all of this and shocked each time I open a card, a letter, an e-mail, or read a post. You have no idea how much you bless my life.

Thanks again,

Shannon

They say behind every good man is a good woman. Well, behind every good woman, there's a good mother, and I truly have the best. At the end of the day, when I've poured everything I have into everyone else, you make sure that I have all my needs met. Thank you for always thinking of me. I don't know where I would be without you.

Prologue

After their annual New Year's party, the girls were optimistic about the year ahead. All of their families were in a good place. Even the Maldonados, who had dealt with some serious issues last semester, were doing much better.

Marisa's brother, Romero, had gotten into some trouble, and their father's sudden outburst during Romero's court appearance had left him incarcerated and facing deportation. If it hadn't been for Shane's father putting his neck on the line, their story would have ended much differently.

Brian Foster had been the driving force behind Mr. Maldonado's release. He had asked for some favors, and now it was Mr. Foster's turn to make good on the promises he had made to some of Port City's most influential people.

And then there was Brandi's father, who had just gotten out of rehab. The Haywoods were all experiencing some difficulties adjusting to his return, but for the most part, they were just happy he was back home and in a good frame of mind.

"I am *not* ready to go back to school," Shane had declared, lying across the bed and dreading the conclusion of Christmas break.

"Me neither. It's too cold outside, and I just want to stay in bed. Christmas break should be as long as summer break. Wouldn't that be nice?" Marisa responded.

"If it wasn't for basketball season, I would just homeschool this semester," Brandi said, laughing.

"Yeah right, we are too fly to be locked up in the house all day," Shane told them. "I wonder what time Ryan's picking me up. I need to text him."

"Dude, how many boyfriends are you gonna have this year?" Brandi asked Shane as they waited for Ryan Petry to pick her up for their date.

"I don't have a boyfriend. Ryan is just a friend who asked me out on a date."

"Um-hm, tell me anything. He is kind of cute, though, in a hot-bookworm kind of way. Ashton is going to be so upset," Brandi chuckled. "Just don't go anyplace where he may see you."

"I am not running from Ashton either. He is just my friend."

"No ... I'm your friend. Marisa's your friend."

"Amen to that!" Marisa hollered from

the bathroom, where she was flat ironing her hair.

"Ryan and Ashton drool when you're anywhere near them. What friends do that?" Brandi asked.

"This is a new year and a new me. I'm just trying to be more open to what's out there. You know I don't really date," Shane told them.

"Oh, so we are on New Year's resolutions now?" Brandi asked.

"I'm down," Marisa hollered from the bathroom. "Gimme a sec." Marisa finished her hair and joined her friends in Shane's bedroom.

"I already know what I have to do this year," Brandi told them. "I have to decide where this thing with Bryce is going. I was so sure before, but now ... I-D-K."

"Yeah, I'm with you, B. Pump your brakes with that one. The thing is, my girl Brandi Haywood can stand on her own two feet. Bryce ain't the reason you still standing ... you are."

Shane knew this was the best moment to tell Brandi how she felt about her relationship with Bryce Thomas. He was a hot-headed kid with a lot of baggage. She had met him in a group for troubled teens, and he was not only troubled, Shane felt he was disturbed.

Brandi nodded her head in agreement. "I know what you're saying, sis. I see it too. Don't think I'm blind."

"Okay, my turn," Marisa told them. "This year I'm focusing on modeling. Somehow, some way, a door is going to open for me. I can just feel it."

"That sounds good to me," Brandi told her. "You've got that *something special*, and somebody's gonna recognize it. You just gotta grind it out. Whatever that means, for wherever you are."

The girls held hands, and each of them

prayed silently for the upcoming year, for their families, and for their goals. Shane stuck her arm out in the middle of the circle. Brandi and Marisa followed suit. "New year, new me," she declared. "Better yet, new year, new we."

"I like that," Marisa said, giving her a nod of approval. "New year, new we."

Brandi repeated it as well, with a smile on her face. "I like it too. Adding it to my timeline today."

"Girl, you need to make a no-Friender resolution," Shane told her. After Brandi's abduction in ninth grade, the girls were all skeptical—and very cautious—about social networking. "You just be careful. And promise us, no Internet dating, please. We just got you back."

"I'm not trying to date anybody, but I like Friender. And that creep, Steven, is not going to have me scared of using my own computer. I won't give him that much power," Brandi declared. "Now let's get back to PCH and rock out the end of this sophomore year."

"That's what I'm talking about," Shane agreed.

CHAPTER 1

Shane

*I*t was cold outside. It had rained for the past two days, so to get a little break from the rain was a pleasant surprise. Today, there wasn't a cloud in the sky. It was a beautiful, crisp winter afternoon. Even the birds had come out to enjoy the sunshine.

Shane wanted to look smart and sophisticated. After all, she knew that Ryan would look like a reporter straight out of the *Port City Tribune* when he arrived. Ryan was a serious twelfth grader, the editor-in-chief of the school newspaper and yearbook, and her boss in her position as photo editor. She wasn't sure what he wanted with a sophomore, but she seemed to intrigue him.

"Hey," Shane said as she jumped into Ryan's Jeep Cherokee. It was an older model, but it was in good shape. She could tell that the radio had been upgraded with an XM system. His truck was comfortable and warm and seemed perfect for him.

"Hey, Shane. I hate to be rude. I should say hello to your parents."

"They aren't even home right now. They had a meeting or something downtown. So no worries. And what do you have planned for us today?"

"You mean Shane Foster is going to let me take the lead on this date? Cool."

"Of course. I know how to ride shotgun."

"Well, in that case, I thought we'd go by the museum for lunch."

"The museum? We are not that old, Ryan. Haven't you heard of burgers and a movie?"

"Girl, didn't you just say that you know how to ride shotgun? Well then, ride."

"You're right, but this better be good. I didn't even know Port City had a museum."

When they arrived at the museum, there was a sign for the current exhibition. It read *Real People, Places, and Faces*, Exhibit Hall B. They followed the directions to Exhibit Hall B, and Shane gasped at the entrance. She looked at Ryan, who watched her as she realized what her eyes were taking in: display after display of work by famous Texas photographers.

Before her was the work of area photographers she admired. The images were powerful. A tribute to the vast Texas landscape. Photographs of aging architecture, old fishing boats, abandoned churches, traditional Mexican weddings, oilmen, cattle ranchers, and rodeos. Quiet photos of mothers and babies. Landscapes of the lone star sky in a series of large panels.

Shane soaked it all in. These artists

were every bit as good as Ansel Adams, Annie Liebovitz, Irving Penn. And these Texans had done it all on film too. She was gobsmacked. She couldn't wrap her brain around film the way she had with digital. It was eye-opening. Mesmerizing. Inspirational. "How did you know this was here? It's everything," she said, never taking her eyes off the work in front of her. "I just wish I had my own camera with me."

Ryan pulled a camera from the bag that he was carrying. "I thought you might say that."

She snapped pictures of the pictures on the wall to document her experience, flash off, of course. By the end of the exhibit, she was emotionally drained. "This was euphoric, Ryan. Thank you so much. I want to come back every day until my own work is on that wall."

"Keep going like you're going and it will be. You have talent, Shane."

Shane couldn't believe that she had never seen Ryan before. Well, she did meet him last year, but she didn't *see* him. This was different. "So what do you have planned for me next?" she asked, more interested than before.

"There's lunch available in the court-yard over there. I was thinking that we could grab some food and a latte or something. They have great shrimp tacos, but you can get whatever you like. You've been a pretty cheap date up until this point," he joked.

"Well, you've been a pretty cheap host, taking me to a free exhibit," she said, nudging him in the side. "But I trust you. If you say the shrimp tacos are great, then I'll give them a shot. You were certainly right about coming to the museum. The exhibit was amazing!"

Shane grabbed a seat in the middle of the courtyard. It was a quaint little area where food carts were lined up and connected by Christmas lights. There were heat lamps in the eating area that kept it nice and toasty.

Shane remembered seeing all kinds of food carts and trucks on her last visit to Austin. The Texas capital had a happening food scene. She saw carts set up in parking lots and on sidewalks—in groups or as stand-alones. They were everywhere. The Fosters had not eaten as well in some of the fancier restaurants in Port City as they had that weekend in Austin. There were gourmet hot dogs, tacos, Vietnamese pho, crepes, cupcakes, puffy tacos, po'boys, gumbo ... You name it, you could find it on a food cart.

And now the carts were popping up all over Port City. But finding them was hit or miss. Who knew the stuffy museum was the place to be for great food? While her hometown had not reached the sophisti-cated heights of Austin, Shane did see a variety of interesting foods to sample in the future. There was a food cart called Oink. And who didn't love pork in all its forms? She made a mental note to try that one later. Another cart seemed to only serve biscuits. And another was called Chill. Homemade ice cream! She was definitely coming back when the temperature warmed up. Her crew was going to eat this up. Literally.

Ryan brought her a white chocolate mocha first so that she could keep warm while her tacos were being prepared. The contrast of the cold air and the hot drink made the steam rise from the cup and dance. The smell of white chocolate tickled her nose. *What an amazing day,* she thought.

Ryan arrived back at the table with their food. The shrimp was blackened to perfection and wrapped in a homemade tortilla filled with cabbage and a secret sauce to die for. "Oh my," Shane said after taking her first bite. "I've never had shrimp tacos this good before."

"Try adding some lime juice."

She squeezed a lime wedge over her taco and took a huge bite. "Why is this so good? Now you're going to have me eating at the museum once a week," she laughed.

"Pretty impressive for little ole Port City, right?" he asked.

"Ryan," she said between bites of taco, "I haven't had food this yummy since my dad took us all to Austin after school got out. They have food carts galore there. I knew we were starting to get some in Port City, but I never thought we'd see anything like this. It's amazing. Brandi and Mari are going to totally flip when I tell them about it."

Shane licked her lips. She looked at Ryan through new eyes. She had seriously misjudged him as geeky and boring. Last year he wasn't even a blip on her radar. But as she peeled back the layers, she saw a guy who had a lot going on.

"Hey, we can hang out here anytime you like. Is your dad ready for the election campaigning to start?"

Just the thought of the election put Shane on pause. "I don't know. I mean, I'm happy for my dad. I'm just nervous. There's a lot about me that you don't know, and I don't want it to be public knowledge either."

"Like what?"

"Nothing, Ryan." There was an awkward silence between them. It had been the first one all day. Ryan regretted bringing up the election. He hadn't wanted to ruin their date.

"I had fun today," he said.

"Me too. Thank you so much. I would have never experienced any of this if it wasn't for you." She could hear her phone vibrating in her purse.

"Wanna hang?" It was a text from Ashton. Her face must have changed because Ryan asked her what was wrong.

"I'm fine," she said. She looked around at where she was. *Ashton would hate it here,* she thought. "Just fine."

"Good, let's get you home. It's getting cold out here."

CHAPTER 2

Marisa

After Mr. Maldonado was released from jail, he tried desperately to get his construction business back up to speed, but his client list was looking very skimpy. Many of his customers switched to his competitors, and he was finding it increasingly difficult to pick up more during the winter when nobody seemed to want to remodel or repair anything. The steady income that flowed into their house wasn't there anymore.

"What are we going to do?" he asked his wife, feeling more nervous than ever.

"Well, first of all, I've added a few new houses to my cleaning service. That should help out a little bit, but I can only clean so much. My hands are starting to ache," she complained to her husband.

"I wouldn't dream of having you take on more than you can handle. I have to find something for myself. That's all."

"You can always try the refinery. I'm sure you can do something there. Can we call somebody?"

"I don't know. They only seem interested in people coming from out of town these days. The climate at the refinery is changing. It's harder to get in, and I hate working for other people. I'm used to having my own business."

"But that's not working for us right now, George. You have to adjust."

"I know. I know."

Marisa could hear everything her parents were saying in the living room. She wasn't trying to eavesdrop. The house was just so quiet today. Their conversation made her nervous. She knew she had to do something to help.

Marisa immediately got online to find out where she could get work. She knew if she obtained a work permit, she could find a job at any of the local fast-food spots. She dreamed of the day when she could make her own money working at a clothing store.

Not only did she love modeling, but she adored fashion. Her passion began years ago when her mother would bring home fashion magazines given to her by her clients. *Vogue*, *Essence*, *Elle*, *Marie Claire* .... They had already been read; it was thoughtful of her mom's clients to pass them on. Why not give them away for someone else to enjoy? And with three daughters at home, Mrs. Maldonado knew they wouldn't go to waste.

Marisa stopped scanning the jobs list the moment her eyes fell on the notice for an open call for models for Gap clothing stores.

"An open call? Right here in Port City?" Marisa said to herself. She knew that she *had* to be there. The date for the open call wasn't until February. That was good. It gave her over a month to prepare. She knew she had to get started right away with eating right and working out.

She was already thin, and she didn't want to look anorexic, but her body could use some toning. And really, Marisa told herself, she could stand to lose a few pounds—since everybody knew the camera added ten. But she wanted to do it in a healthy way.

Her head was in the clouds, dreaming about the day of the open call. She had visions of showing up and being whisked past the other girls who had been waiting for hours. She'd be discovered on the spot and moved to the front of the line.

She knew she had to assemble the perfect outfit. She needed to look like she had just stepped out of a Gap ad. She was a girl on a mission. She was determined for it to work out, not only for her but for her family.

CHAPTER 3

Brandi

"Everyone, please take out your protractors now," Mr. Mutomba instructed the class. He drew a half circle on the board and marked off angles, labeling them obtuse, right, and acute. "I'll need you to be able to differentiate these three types of angles. You'll have a quiz over this lesson on Friday."

"Com 2 rr," flashed on Brandi's phone. It was Bryce. Her face lit up at the anticipation of getting away from this boring lesson and going to see her boo. Her hand shot up in the air as soon as she read it.

"Yes, Brandi, you have a question,"

Mr. Mutomba asked in his thick African accent.

"Yes, sir, may I please be excused to go to the restroom. It's an emergency."

"Just take the restroom pass off my desk. Anymore questions at this time?" he asked, scanning the room. "Okay, turn to page three fifty-six in your text. There are ten practice questions on that page. You'll be responsible for all of them."

Brandi could hear his instructions as she left the room. She rolled her eyes, knowing that she would have to make up the assignment when she returned. It was enough to make her not want to come back at all.

"Hey, you," she said as she approached Bryce in the empty hallway. His face always made her pause. He was absolutely gorgeous. *How did I get so lucky?* she thought. This kid was naturally tanned and had the most amazing curly hair. His Dickies were starched and sagged just the right amount. The contrast of his light blue polo against his skin gave Brandi butterflies.

He was such a pretty boy. And Brandi had a weakness for the pretty ones. She knew she had a type. But she had also learned that she was not the best judge of character. As she took in the eye candy, her heart thumped away. But red flags were trying to wake up her sluggish head.

It was too soon to be with anyone, and she knew it. But she dismissed those silly thoughts as soon as they came up. Bryce was exactly what she needed. At least that's what she wanted to believe. "What took you so long?" he asked, agitated.

"Here we go. I was in *class*, Bryce. I had to get permission to leave. You should have sent the text *before* you left class instead of from the restroom."

"Girl, watch your mouth! Don't tell me what I should have done. Just get your big behind out here when I text you."

"Whatever, Bryce, I don't even know why I left class for you. You make me sick," she huffed. She folded her arms and dug her heels into the floor. She was not going to give in to this boy.

"Oh, I make you sick, huh? Girl, you know you love me. Now come give me a kiss before my teacher gets mad that I've been gone so long."

"I don't wanna kiss yo' stank behind, Bryce."

"Yeah, you do," he said, pulling her close to him. Even though she didn't want to, she melted in his arms. "See, I told you," he said breathlessly. He kissed her like she belonged to him, and she loved every moment. "Now next time, don't keep me waiting," he said, slapping her on the butt.

"Boy, stop," she said right as the assistant principal came around the corner.

"Is there a problem here?" he asked Brandi.

"No, sir. I was just heading back to class. I had to use the restroom."

"Good," he said, giving Bryce the once-over.

Everyone was a little more protective of Brandi since her abduction last spring. Mr. Spears was no different. The school had held candlelight vigils. Counselors had been called in to deal with emotional students. Her photograph had been plastered all over the campus.

"Where are you headed, son?" Mr. Spears asked.

"I'm not your son," Bryce said, snapping at Mr. Spears. "I am going to class."

"Fair enough, young man, but talking to people the way you do tells me that whoever *does* claim you as a son isn't teaching you much at home."

Brandi braced herself. She knew that Mr. Spears had hit Bryce's weak spot: his parents.

"What did you say?" Bryce asked slowly.

Brandi tried to stop him. "Come on, Bryce. Let's go to class. Bye, Mr. Spears," she said, pulling Bryce down the hall.

"Girl! Let go of me," he told her.

"No, you are going to class before you get in trouble. Bryce! Look at me! You have to chill. I know what he said pushed your buttons, but he's the assistant principal. Chill!" she said, looking him eye-to-eye.

"I'ma chill now, but it ain't over with that fool," he warned her.

Brandi was getting tired of trying to save him from himself. She felt like her mother. It was the same thing that she was trying to do with her dad, save him from himself.

"I know, baby," she said, giving him a peck on the lips to calm him down.

As soon as she returned to class, Brandi began gathering her things. Mr. Mutomba checked the clock and shook his head.

"Miss Haywood," he said, "I expect you to turn in those ten practice questions tomorrow."

Just then, the bell rang. Mr. Mutomba approached her as she tried to slink out of the room. "What took you so long? You missed a great deal of instruction."

"I'm sorry, Mr. Mutomba. I had feminine problems," she said and smiled, showing her beautiful white teeth. She could tell she'd made her teacher uncomfortable, and she felt a little twinge of guilt watching his reaction.

"Oh ... okay ... carry on, then," he said nervously.

CHAPTER 4

Campaign Kickoff

The Pier was a plush room donned with chandeliers, a dining area, a full chef's kitchen, and a posh seating area with soft couches designed for mingling. It was the perfect location for Mr. Foster's announcement party. It would be the first fundraiser of his campaign. Everyone who was anyone in the city had been invited. Outfits had been purchased by Mrs. Foster for Robin, Shane, and Aiden. They looked like the picture-perfect family. Standing in front of their friends and family, nobody would have known that their home had been a chaotic nightmare only hours before.

"I'm not wearing that stupid dress," Shane told her mother. "Where did you buy that anyway, Sears?"

"Shane, just wear the dress. You'll look fine," Robin told her. "Plus, Mom has us all in the same colors, so it'll look good when we're all together. This is about Dad, not you."

"Shane, I'm warning you, put the dress on before you make us late," her mother scolded her.

Shane looked at the clothes in disgust. There was no personality, and everyone was too matchy-matchy in navy blue and red. Who would wear that? All she needed were white gloves and little Sunday hat to complete her nerd look.

"You have us dressed like dweebs, and I'm not looking like that in front of my friends. No way."

"What's the problem?" her dad shouted, catching her off guard.

"Nothing, I'm just not wearing this dress. Look at me, Dad. If I have to wear it, then I'm not going."

"All of this is over a dress? You have to be kidding me. I'm a nervous wreck, and I have to break up an argument over clothing. Put the dress on now or else you won't see the light of day when this is over. Am I clear?" His voice was growing louder, but Shane still didn't respond. When she got into one of her moods, there was no reasoning with her. "Am I clear, Shane?" he yelled.

"Huh?" She had used that word since she was two years old. When asked a question that she didn't want to answer, *huh* was her go-to response.

"Don't play with me, Shane," Mr. Foster

had warned her and left the room. He knew continuing to argue with her would get them nowhere, but she knew when he returned that dress had better be on her body.

All eyes were on the Foster family that day. While Brian Foster was busy mingling with his guests, all of the major news stations were arriving. They were all prepared to document his run for the Area 14 seat. Hundred dollar bills were being put in his hands as he moved through the crowd, shaking hands with his guests. "You and your family are a great representation of our city, Mr. Foster," Joann Marks, a former council member, told him, pulling out her checkbook. She wrote a five hundred dollar check.

"Mrs. Marks, this is too much."

"Honey, it's never too much, especially when you are running against a snake like Stringer," she said in her perfect southern drawl. She had been on the council for years but gave up her seat when her husband became ill.

You would have never known she was eighty-two years old. She was a tall, regal older lady with impeccably styled salt-and-pepper hair. In her former life, she was a businesswoman. She and her husband owned a thriving swimming pool company. With time on her hands, she became a motivational speaker, and that took on a life of its own. She was still one of Port City's most sought-after speakers. When her husband was diagnosed with cancer, they decided it was time to slow down, travel, and enjoy each other.

Now, the only politics that she involved herself with was giving, and she was very generous. "If you ever need anything, Mr. Foster, please do not hesitate to call me."

Brian Foster was surprised he had so much support, but not as surprised as his family.

"Is Dad going to be famous now?" Shane asked Robin.

"You are so young sometimes. Yeah, sure, he'll be famous in Port City."

"Well, dang, I'm famous too, then."

"Go talk to Marisa and Brandi. Your conversations are stupid."

"You're stupid. Give me Aiden. I want my nephew." Shane went from table to table talking to her friends. Marisa, Brandi, Trent, and Ashton sat at one table, and Ryan and most of the journalism department were one table over. Shane stopped to talk to her friends from journalism first.

"Is this your nephew?" one of the girls gushed.

"Yeah, this is Aiden." He smiled that beautiful Foster smile, showing his gums.

"Hey, I didn't want to have them just start taking pictures without your permission, but we can get some great shots for the campaign if you like," Ryan told her.

"That sounds great, Ryan. You are awesome," she said, hugging him.

Ashton's ears immediately perked up when he heard Shane. He knew Ryan was making a move in her direction, and he was upset that she was even entertaining the idea of dating him. Ashton and Ryan had been in the same classes since middle school. They were two totally different people, and he just couldn't believe he was competing with *him* for Shane's attention.

By the time Shane arrived at her best friends' table, heat was rising off of Ashton, making him uncharacteristically quiet.

"Hey, hey, hey … where my peoples at?" she asked, joking with her friends. Ashton immediately got up from the table and walked to the other room. "What's with your boy?" she asked Trent.

"You know what's with him," Trent told her.

"Girl, what you wearing?" Brandi

snorted. "Looks like your mom went to Gymboree for teenagers."

"Hey, now," Shane started to say, then she rolled her eyes. "I was threatened. I could stay in the house forever, or wear this stupid sack. Here, take Aiden for a second," she said to Marisa.

"Hey, why does she get to keep Aiden," Brandi complained, but Shane was already gone and trying to find Ashton.

She searched the seating area, but he was nowhere to be found. She peeked in every nook and cranny in the whole building, but she couldn't find him. Just when she was about to give up, she noticed him pass by the door. He was outside and heading toward his car.

"Ash, where are you going? Come back inside. It's freezing out here."

"Nah, I'm good, Shane. Go back in there with your dude and them."

"What?" she asked, confused.

"Ryan Petry, you know who I'm talking about. Stop playing, Shane."

"It's not like that, Ashton," she whined. She didn't even know why she was standing in the cold trying to reason with him. She hadn't made a commitment to either one of them, but she still had drama.

"Look, I know that we ain't like that. You don't have to be out here trying to make me feel better. It's all good, Shane," he said, taking both of her hands in his. "I'm the one with the problem. I was the one who started wanting you, not the other way around."

"Ash, I'm sorry. I don't know what to say. Things may be different if I was looking to be wifed, but that's not where I'm at right now."

"So, are you telling Nerd Alert in there the same thing?" he asked, looking down at her intently.

"Don't be mean or nosy," she said,

dropping his hands. "Now come back in and get out of your feelings."

"Ah, you got jokes. I'm not in my feelings."

They never saw Ryan in the doorway as he watched the two of them holding hands. He knew that he had to step up his game. There was no girl who interested him as much as Shane Foster, and he was determined not to let her get away.

CHAPTER 5

Shane

Argh, I hate biology, and more than anything, I hate Mrs. Smith, Shane thought as she arrived at her third period class.

"Good morning, Shane," Mrs. Smith said with a huge smile on her face.

"Good morning," Shane responded, thoroughly confused. This woman was not one to speak, much less do it in a cheerful voice. Some of the other students looked at Shane curiously. They had occasionally witnessed an exchange of words between Shane and Mrs. Smith. They just didn't get along, but today she acted as if Shane was her favorite student.

Mrs. Smith already had their drill on the overhead when they walked into class. The state examination was coming up, so every teacher seemed to be focused on it. The only good thing about her class was the fact that Mrs. Smith only made them study for the test during the daily drill. After that, it was business as usual. All of it was a snoozefest for Shane. She knew science was really important. But she couldn't geek out. Science wasn't her thing.

Mrs. Smith made her usual stroll around the classroom, checking for homework. *Shoot, shoot, shoot,* Shane thought. *I forgot about my homework with all of the commotion at my house this weekend.*

"Shane, did you complete your homework?" Mrs. Smith asked her.

"No, Mrs. Smith. I had a really busy weekend. Honestly—"

Mrs. Smith stopped her where she was. She bent down to whisper in Shane's ear, which surprised the heck out of Shane. Their relationship had never been familiar enough for her to do that. If it had been Mrs. Monroe, then it would be different. This was Mrs. Smith, who was pegged as one of the scariest teachers in the school.

Shane could smell the activator Mrs. Smith used in her hair as she bent down. Mrs. Smith was one of the few people Shane knew who still wore a curl in her hair. In the eighties, many African American women wore curls. They were new and hip then. It made black hair curly and manageable. But it was very difficult to maintain. Most people had moved on to other styles.

In the 2000s, it was hard to find anyone who still used or sold the product. And then there was Mrs. Smith, who found the one person on the planet who could hook her up. "Shane, I saw you and your family on the news last night. I know it must have been a busy weekend for you. When is a good time for you to turn your assignment in to me?"

Huh, she's asking me? This is a first. "Well I could have it to you by the end of the day," Shane told her, still a bit confused as to what was happening.

"Tomorrow is fine, but don't make a habit out of it."

"Yes, ma'am." Shane thought she had died and landed in Bizarroland. *Too many chemicals in the biology room is driving this woman crazy.*

When Shane left from third period, it was time for lunch. She headed to her usual table to wait for Brandi and Marisa. Mrs. Smith had been so weird. She just had to share it with her besties. She spotted them at the salad bar and decided to join them. "Hey, you can't just cut in line," one of the girls at the end told her.

"Um, yeah, she kinda can," Brandi

responded as she made room for Shane to put together her salad.

"Thanks, B. How's y'all's day going?" she asked.

"Crazy slow. Wishing it was over," Brandi told her.

"I'm tired after your dad's announcement party last night. I just want to go to bed," Marisa told her.

"Yeah, well, my day was crazy," Shane told them. She told them how Mrs. Smith had treated her, and how she gave her an extra few hours on her homework. They were stunned.

"Girl, you know she's all political and stuff," Brandi told her.

"No, I had no clue."

"Yep, one time, when my mom went to vote, she was working the polls. She was all trying to get my mom to vote for some guy."

"Oh, now that explains it," Shane said as the lightbulb finally went off.

The girls sat down at the table with their salads and bottles of water. The new year had been an inspiration for all of them to start making healthier choices in their diets. They were trying to stick to it at school as well as at home.

While they were nibbling on their salads and chatting, the principal was making rounds in the cafeteria. "Good afternoon, ladies."

"Hi, Mrs. Montgomery," they all said.

"Well, you ladies must be exhausted. I caught a peek of you on the news last night. What time did your dad's announcement party end?" she asked Shane.

"I'm really not sure, Mrs. Montgomery. I just know I'm tired."

"Well, if you need to lie down in the nurse's office, be my guest. That goes for all of you. We are going to try to help you get through the election. It may be a tiring journey, but we will do what we can to help you."

"Thanks, Mrs. Montgomery," Shane said. "We really appreciate it."

"Oh, and, Shane, please tell your father that I think he will do our city proud. I live in Area 14, and he definitely has my vote."

By the end of the day, it was apparent to Shane that everybody in Port City knew or was about to find out that her father was running for office. Before he had decided to run, she really hadn't given much thought to city politics. There was a whole world going on in Port City that she had no idea about.

This day had been like no other day at PCH. Shane had a feeling there would be many more days like this. She knew change was coming for her family. She could feel it in the air.

CHAPTER 6

Marisa

The day of the Gap open call had finally arrived. Marisa had Trent bring her to the mall early that morning. She wanted to be one of the first people in line so she wouldn't look tired by the time she met with the casting agents. She was disappointed when she arrived and the line was out the door and growing by the second. The teenage hopefuls were plentiful, and the line had begun to wrap around the building.

"Do you want me to wait with you?"

Trent asked as he pulled his truck up to the end of the line.

"Nah, I'm good. I brought my tablet with me. I'm just going to download a new book or something. Don't worry about me. I'm in it for the long haul."

"Well, call me if you need anything. Hey," he stopped her before she could get out, "you lookin' right."

He made her blush. She climbed back in the huge Hummer truck and planted a kiss on his lips. It seemed that everybody was staring at her. It was making her feel awkward.

She definitely looked the part of a Gap model. She wore a pair of skinny jeans and a relaxed-fit white tee that hung off her shoulders, but in her bag she brought a spring outfit that would work perfectly with the brown riding boots she wore. And with the pair of polka dot flats she also had in her bag, she was ready for anything. She had a change of makeup, a change of clothing, snacks, and entertainment for herself. The only thing she hadn't brought was a chair. She never thought that she'd be so far back in the line.

Marisa definitely hadn't anticipated the amount of competition that would be there—people didn't stop adding to the line! The guys who showed up didn't bother her. It was the number of girls she would have to compete with that made her edgy. They were all so different.

What is the casting panel looking for? she wondered. She took out her tablet and began to study recent Gap ads. What was the look? What were they missing? And where could she fit?

She was jolted back to reality by a very attractive male who was helping with casting. "We need to get your picture," he informed her. His assistant took a Polaroid picture of her, and she was given an application to be completed before she made it to the front of the line.

It took two hours, but she finally made it to the door. She used her tablet to take a picture of herself in front of the door where the Gap casting sign was located. As soon as she posted her picture onto Friender, the Internet went nuts. Her friends immediately began to send notes of encouragement to her timeline.

Marisa saw a row of tables when she made it inside the door. A stylish young woman asked her for her application and the Polaroid picture that Marisa had been over-analyzing since it had been taken outside.

Once her paperwork was okayed, she was given a number and told to wait in one of the chairs that lined the wall.

Marisa sat down and took a deep breath. She had finally made it inside. *Now what happens next?*

Marisa took it all in. Where the Gap casting call was set up was the area the mall reserved for holiday events or promotions—like pictures with Santa or the Easter Bunny. Today there were five tables arranged in a semi-circle. At each table were two people. Marisa assumed one was a casting rep from the Gap and the other was their assistant.

One of the reps was constantly glancing over at her. Even while he was interviewing other potential models! He was making her nervous. *I really don't want to wind up at his table*, she thought.

"Hey." A young black girl with smoky gray eyes sat next to Marisa. Her naturally curly hair reminded her of Shane.

"Hey," Marisa said back to her.

"You nervous?" she asked.

"Not really. I have my moments, I guess, like at the entrance. The butterflies in my stomach started dancing."

"Girl, who you telling? Me too. I couldn't even sleep last night. I had to drive in from Bay City. We don't get many auditions where I live."

"Yeah, well, there aren't usually any in Port City either, but here we are."

"I'm Ella."

"Marisa. Nice to meet you. So have you modeled before?"

"My mom's had me modeling since I was two. I did a lot of ads for the local stores in Bay City, but nothing like Gap, ya know?"

"Wow. That's impressive. I've never been in any ads, not even locally."

"Is this your first audition?"

"Yeah."

"Well, welcome to the industry. You have the look, in my opinion. I'm sure you'll be around for a long time."

"Next, number two seventy-four!" the announcer called over the microphone.

"Well, that's me," Marisa told her new friend.

"Hey, are you on Friender?" Ella asked.

"Yeah, Marisa Maldonado. Don't forget to friend me."

"Doing it right now. Ella Pearson. Just in case it doesn't work."

"Good luck, Ella," Marisa said right before she was ushered beyond the ropes to where the casting reps sat. To her dismay, she was sent to the very rep who kept glancing her way. He made her uneasy. *Is it a coincidence that I'm at his table?* she wondered. She had to put any uncomfortable thoughts out of her mind in order to turn on her inner fabulousness. And she did, after all, *want* these people to like her appearance. She should be happy about the attention.

"You are Marisa Maldonado?" the female assistant sitting next to the casting rep asked her.

"Yes, ma'am. My friends call me Mari. I have three younger siblings. I'm a good student, and I'm driven. I'm young, but I know my worth," she said, feeling confident and secure. She wasn't sure where all of that came from, but it was as if she just knew how to read what they wanted, the wholesome, confident girl next door.

"So, why should we choose you out of all of the people in this room?" asked the man who had been looking at her. She shook off her nerves. She could do this. As she started to speak, she looked directly into his eyes.

"I am what Gap is missing. Most of the girls who look like they *might* be Hispanic in the ads make you wonder, is she Hispanic or white? With me, you'd know. When a young Hispanic girl flips through a magazine and sees an ad with my picture, I'll inspire her."

"You are not as tall as some of the other girls here. How tall are you?" the assistant asked, seeing if her confidence would waiver.

"I'm five seven, but what I lack in height, I make up for in every other way. I'm confident, secure, motivated, and ready," she assured the rep and his assistant.

The Gap representatives seemed to be impressed. She was given an orange ticket to move on to the next phase of casting. On the inside, she was doing back handsprings, but in front of the casting panel, she politely thanked them and went into the area designated for phase-two applicants. She posted on Friender that she was on to the next round of auditions, where she would compete with the best of the best. Everyone was excited for her.

When she saw Ella again, she was being ushered into the room as well, orange ticket in hand. "Well, we made it to the next round," Ella said excitedly. "Congrats on your first open call. It's huge to get past the first cut."

"Yeah, I'm excited. What time do you think we'll start round two? What are we going to do?"

"It kind of depends. No two auditions are ever the same." They waited for another thirty minutes before a panel of three casting reps arrived in the room.

A beautiful lady with a charming English accent greeted them. "Congratulations on making it this far in the process. First give yourselves a round of applause because one of you will be representing Texas in our next ad campaign.

"We're launching a state-to-state advertising campaign, and one of the first five states we'll focus on will be Texas. Today, we will have a small photo shoot. The five best pictures will compete with the other Texas hopefuls. Ultimately, we will choose one guy and one girl to represent your state.

"We should know who our models are in the next month or so. We will contact you via e-mail and phone. Any questions about round two? ... Great, then let's get started."

Marisa looked around the room at her competition. Everyone was absolutely gorgeous. They had weeded through the people who had come to the audition just because it was an open call and got down to the people with potential. *I am out of my league,* Marisa thought, looking around, but she quickly put the negativity out of her mind.

When it was her turn for her mini photo shoot, she nailed it. She knew her face and her angles, and she knew how to manipulate the camera. Her poses were deliberate but they looked effortless; her photos turned out versatile and inviting. The photographer loved her.

For the first pictures, she wore her jeans and off-the-shoulder white tee. As the shoot went on, she began to layer her clothing using the accessories she'd brought. First she added a scarf, and then she added a sweater for a nice fall look. The orange sweater contrasted beautifully with her naturally tanned skin.

When it was over, the photographer

thanked her and showed her the photos he thought were best. She had never been photographed by a professional before. The pictures were amazing. She couldn't believe that it was actually her. She *had* to win this job. She had never wanted anything more in her life.

CHAPTER 7

Brandi

*E*ver since Brandi returned home, things in her family had been on a better path. Her father blamed himself and his drug addiction for Brandi's willingness to connect to a stranger on the Internet. He thought it was the reason for her abduction. Brandi knew in her heart that he was right. If she was able to get the love she needed from him, then she probably never would have been so gullible.

What would my life be like if my father was never an addict? she wondered. She didn't know who she would be if he wasn't who he was. Now he was back and every-thing was supposed to be business as usual, but there was still uncertainty their home.

They all knew that their lives were much different than those of their friends and neighbors. They had to deal with the ugly face of addiction. Other families seemed to take it for granted how good they had it. Drugs abuse affected almost every decision that the Haywoods made.

Brandi could tell that her mother was struggling with her father's return. She was picking up double shifts to make ends meet. He was trying to play Mr. Mom, but he wasn't really good at it.

"You need to be out looking for a job, James. I want to spend more time with the girls. I can't continue to pull double shifts at the hospital. You have to pull your own weight around here."

"Dang, Cat, okay. Stop riding me all the time. I'm doing the best I can right now.

My homeboy is going to hook me up with a job at the plant. I just have to wait until they have something."

"You always looking for somebody to hook yo' black behind up. Get out there and get it on your own," she replied, disgusted at his lack of ambition.

Brandi's mother blamed herself for a lot of things. She had missed much of Brandi's formative years. And those times were so critical for young women. Mothers had to be vigilant with their daughters. You couldn't just tune out. But that's exactly what Mrs. Haywood felt she did.

She spent so many hours working, trying to keep her family afloat. Her remaining time was spent mopping up after her drug-addicted husband. When she wasn't worried about whether he was coming home or not, she was cleaning up vomit or trying to keep him hidden from his daughters when he was high as a kite.

She vowed that they were not going to

mess up Raven the way they had messed up Brandi. This round of rehab had better stick or she didn't know what would happen.

"I ain't looking for no hookups all the time. Oh, maybe Brian Foster knows if they're hiring at the city. I'ma talk to him tomorrow," Brandi's dad replied.

Catherine Haywood fell back into her thoughts. She was a bundle of nerves, but she wasn't going to show that side of herself to anyone. She didn't want to push her husband too hard. She didn't want to be the reason he relapsed. But inside, she was screaming at him and trying to make him understand that calling Brian was the same as waiting on a hookup from his "homeboy."

Surely he had heard of job boards and monster.com, but James Haywood had to be ushered into a position. He couldn't just find a job like a normal person. He had come from an upstanding family and had been a spoiled youngest son. Now his wife was left with a mess of a husband.

She knew that their girls needed their father, so she had to help him get through this. It was the only way they would meet the man that she had fallen in love with so many years ago in college. Before the drugs.

Time went by. She had finished school while he had smoked weed and dropped out. That should have been a red flag, but she was too in love to admit that he had a problem.

The arguments in the Haywood home weren't aggressive. There were no broken plates or holes in the wall; however, they were still far from a perfect household. Brandi knew her parents were on the right track. There had been real improvement. But she longed for the family environment that Shane or Marisa had. Their homes seemed "perfectly flawed."

All families had their problems, she knew that. Her family's problems seemed extraordinary. There was never anything ordinary about being an addict. Not only did the individual suffer, but the family suffered too. Brandi had heard that addiction was a selfish disease, and the truth of that was now becoming clear to her.

When she was younger, she wasn't able to understand her mother, but now she was beginning to. Catherine Haywood was alone too. Brandi and Raven had been fatherless during the really rough times, but their mother was husbandless. Husbandless with a husband was one of the worst things a woman could be. Brandi was determined to not follow in her mother's footsteps on that one.

Her boyfriend, Bryce, was obviously not the caring and consoling individual that Brandi had dreamed he would be. His mother's addiction left him just as scarred as she was feeling. She couldn't get the little stunt he pulled at school out of her mind. It was a red flag.

He was volatile. She couldn't keep on excusing his behavior. It was always the same thing. After he got angry, he cozied up to her to make it all better. She fell for it every time. It wasn't until she was alone in her room that she could admit to herself what a fool she was. She was more like her mother than she realized. Otherwise she would have dumped him the first time he lost his cool.

One thing she had learned from her kidnapping was to trust her instincts, and they were telling her to get out while the getting was good.

CHAPTER 8

Dodging Cupid's Arrow

"I hate Valentine's Day!" Shane announced as she joined her two best friends at their lockers. "It's so cheesy."

"You just mad 'cause you're not in love right now," Brandi told her.

"This is my favorite holiday," Marisa said, smiling. "Especially since I have Trent." Marisa did a quick twirl in the hallway, her hands covering her heart.

"Yeah, well, I don't want any part of

the dance this weekend. Well, I'm going to be there, but just to get some pics for the newspaper."

"Get one of those geeky people you hang around on yearbook committee to do that so you and Ashton can roll with me and Trent. He asked if you had a date yet," Marisa said, warning her that he was interested in taking her.

"He called hinting at the fact that he wanted to take me, but Ryan asked too. I'm not ready to go to the Valentine's dance with either one of them. It seems like it could be taken the wrong way."

"Only Shane would have two dates for the dance and choose neither," Brandi retorted. "You want me to see if Bryce has a friend or something, then it won't be so major of a decision?"

"I guess y'all not understanding that I don't want to go at all—with anybody."

They exited the building to look for Robin. It was Tuesday night. There was a basketball home game. The girls were headed to catch a bite to eat at Jerry's before the game. The Port City High Wildcats were playing the Texas City High Tigers, whose team was having a great year. The anticipation for the game had been building on Friender, where both teams were going back-and-forth, debating who would be the ultimate winner.

"Did you talk to Trent today?" Shane asked Marisa. "Is he ready for the game tonight? The Tigers have been talking so much trash. We have to win."

"Girl, Trent is always ready. My man is the truth."

They heard giggles behind them as Marisa made her declaration. It was Ashley Rivera again. Marisa had attempted to be friends with Ashley after years of beefing, but when she caught her shamelessly flirting with Trent, she knew that she had to get her out of her life for good. Now here she was trying to cause problems where no problems existed. Marisa was determined not to fall for it again.

"What you laughing at?" Brandi asked, welcoming one of Ashley's little friends to jump fly.

"Nothing, we were just saying the same thing, and we thought it was ironic," Ashley told them.

"And what would that be?" Shane asked defensively.

"I was just saying that Trent was the truth too. If I wasn't dating Dalton, it'd be a different story."

"Are you serious right now, Ashley?" Marisa asked, taking the bait. "I'm the one who hooked you up with Dalton, and he don't even want yo' trifling behind." Dalton and Ashley had double dated with Marisa and Trent, but he just wasn't into her and Marisa knew it. Dalton Broussard, power forward for PCH, could have any girl he wanted, and Ashley wasn't it.

"If he didn't want me, then why would

he be taking me to the Valentine's dance this weekend?" she asked sarcastically.

"Maybe because he wants somebody who's down to be trampish ... like you," Shane said calmly and walked away from the mayhem to flag down her sister.

"Oh no you didn't! I don't get down like that!" Ashley shouted. She ran after Shane, getting in her face.

"Yeah, right, Ashley. That's not what Dalton told me last year when he was all up on me and every other girl at this school. Everybody knows what Dalton is about. And quite frankly," Shane said, lowering her voice to a whisper and leaning toward Ashley, "they all know what you're about too."

Ashley's arm flew back in an attempt to slap Shane across the face, but Shane saw it coming and had her by the throat before she could make contact. Ashley's face turned as red as the Valentine hearts that decorated the fence that Shane threw her up against. "You ain't 'bout that life, Ashley. I've been wishing you would step to me. Don't make that mistake again," she warned her as Ashley tried to regain her composure.

"Have fun at the dance," Marisa shouted back, laughing as they jumped in the car with Robin and Aiden.

"You did Ashley so wrong," Brandi said, laughing as they got in the car.

"I know, but she was about to slap me. What else could I do?" Shane asked innocently.

"Oh no, what happened?" Robin asked.

Brandi gave her the whole story in her usual animated way. They laughed at Ashley and her weak little crew that did nothing to come to her aid. "I can't believe they just stood there," Robin said.

"They saw the looks our faces and opted out of that one," Brandi told them. "It would have been three on three, and they knew we'd had enough of Ashley's mouth. I don't think they were willing to take the hit for her on that one."

"I was so ready, and you know I'm not a fighter, but Ashley is just a disrespectful little witch. I tried to be nice to her. I really did," Marisa told them.

"You did," Shane said to her.

"That's a couple of days of your life you can never get back. What a waste," Brandi told her.

They arrived at Jerry's and ordered their food. Brandi had to be back at school with the cheerleaders in one hour, so they had to eat quickly.

"Hey, let me hold Aiden while y'all eat," Marisa told them.

"Here we go again. That Gap audition better not have you starving yourself."

"No, I'm not, but my appetite is slim to none. I just want to hear back from them so badly. They did send an e-mail telling me that I was one of the finalists," she said as a smile crept to her face.

"What?! You didn't even tell us! Does Trent know?" They all began talking at once.

"I haven't told anybody," she admitted. "I didn't want to jinx it, but I couldn't hold it in any longer."

"That's so awesome, Mari," Robin told her, giving her a huge hug as they squeezed Aiden between them.

As soon as they were done stuffing their faces, they headed to the game. Brandi went to the gym to meet the cheerleaders, and Shane went to work taking pictures. Marisa and Robin found a seat right behind the basketball team, but close enough to the aisle so that Robin could get to the restroom if Aiden had to be changed.

Aiden's father, Gavin, joined the girls shortly after they sat down to help Robin with the baby. Even though they had both graduated the year before, they loved attending the games. Basketball was huge in Port City and gained support from almost half the community.

When the Wildcats hit the court, the crowd went crazy. The Tigers team hadn't come alone, though. Many of their fans had come to support them, but there was nothing like home-court advantage.

Trent threw his favorite towel to Marisa as he passed by her and Robin. It was his way of letting her know that he was thinking about her.

Unfortunately, the Wildcat's entrance would turn out to be the most exciting part of the evening. By halftime, everybody realized it was going to be a snoozefest.

The Tigers had gained a lot of clout in their area, but they were no match for the Wildcats' zone defense or for Trent's fast breaks. After Trent's second slam dunk, he was benched by Coach Mac along with Ashton and Dalton. The second string players had taken their place on the court, and that left the first string to chill until the game was over.

The Tigers had talked a lot of noise on Friender, but when they came to PCH, it was a blowout. The Tigers' fans started to leave before the game was over. By the end of fourth quarter, the only people left in the stands were Wildcats' fans.

The PCH fans probably would have left too if it wasn't Valentine's week. Rumor had it that many players on the basketball team were still without dates. The girls flocked to the court when the game was over.

Shane busied herself with her photography in the bleachers. It took her by surprise when her lens fell on Ashton talking to one of Ashley's friends, Courtney Bernard. Courtney was one of the girls who was with Ashley when Shane almost beat her down. *Nice try,* Shane thought.

She slowly relocated to the court area where she could get a better look at what was going on. Ashton put his number in Courtney's phone, and she added her number to his. Shane knew that something was going on; she just had to find out what.

As soon as Courtney walked away, she zoomed her camera in on Ashton as he tied his shoes on the bench. "That's the best look you got for me, Ashton?" she hollered.

"Hey, there she is! You get some good pics of me with that thing?" he asked.

"You wanna see?" she asked, handing him the camera. He scrolled through the pictures, but the only ones on there were of him and Courtney. "Y'all lookin' all couple cute and stuff," she joked.

He smacked his lips. "Nah, it ain't like that. We just going to the Valentine's dance together."

"You're taking Courtney," she paused, "to the Valentine's dance? C'mon."

"Don't act like that. You know I wanna go with you. You're *making* me go with her."

"I can't make you do anything, fool."

"Tell me you'll come with me and she's history."

Out of the corner of her eye, she saw Ryan as he entered the gym. He looked like he was looking for somebody. *Dang, I know he's looking for me,* she thought. *And he's going to see me talking to Ashton.*

He raised himself on his toes and gestured to someone. He was talking to the only white girl on the cheerleading squad. She ran over to talk to him, pompoms shaking. Shane felt sick to her stomach. *What the heck is going on today?*

"Shane?" Ashton asked, confused. "Earth to Shane," he said, following her gaze to Ryan. "Oh, it's good, Shane. You go see nerdy boy and hit me later."

"Wait, what? Ashton?" She tried to get

his attention, but he was gone. "Shoot," she said to herself and went to find her friends.

The day of the Valentine's dance was rainy and cold. It was by no means weather to be out in little dresses trying to look cute. Shane was happy she had opted out of going to the dance. She put on warm-ups, a cozy green sweater, her brown Uggs, and a cute polka-dot knit hat that she slipped over her unruly mane.

She looked like a true photographer as she slipped through the cafeteria door. There were only two other students there to take pictures. They divided the work into sections and prepared for the task of completing this week's newspaper.

When Ashley, Dalton, Courtney, and Ashton walked into the dance, they stood in her section right by the refreshment table. She was supposed to be getting pictures of them, but she just couldn't do it. She would never immortalize that little group.

She was so relieved when she saw Brandi walk through the door. She had to admit her girl was looking cute. Her thick hair was pulled into a tight bun on the top of her head, and her makeup was flawless. Brandi's skin looked as smooth as melted chocolate. Bryce was close behind her with his hand on the small of her back. *He's so controlling. I hate that loser,* Shane thought as she walked over to greet her friend. "You look hot, B," she said, giving her a hug. "Let me get some pics of y'all."

Brandi and Bryce posed for the camera, looking like the cutest couple ever. Brandi's dark chocolate skin and his caramel color blended together perfectly. *Too bad looks ain't everything,* Shane thought.

"Hold up, hold up! My girl done entered the building. It's America's Next Top Model," Shane announced, snapping Marisa's picture as she walked through the door. Marisa halfheartedly protested the attention from her BFF. Shane looked at the shots she took of Marisa in her camera. "Girl, you've been studying your angles. You make me look like a pro."

"You know baby got it like that," Trent said, kissing her on the lips. She wiped the residue of lip gloss off his lips. Anybody looking could see they were in love. They made such a ruckus at the entrance of the cafeteria that people were starting to turn and stare. Ashton came rushing over to talk to Trent. "Big T! My dude."

"Ash! Where my ninja at?"

"Them girls have Dalton on a tight leash. They mad that we wanted to come over here, something about Shane." He turned his attention to her. "What you do to Ashley the other day?"

"I don't know what you talking about," she lied.

"She choked her!" Brandi jumped in.

"Is that why Courtney asked me to

come to the dance? To piss you off? I feel used, but I'ma let her use me all night," he jokingly said, dancing to the music.

"You working or playing?" She heard a rough voice behind her. She knew it was Ryan.

She turned around and stepped back so that he could see her clothes. Even in her Uggs and warm-ups, she was confident. All the girls around her were made up like little porcelain dolls, and there she stood, casual and comfortable. Most girls would have cared, but not Shane.

"Don't I look like I'm working?" she asked him.

"Looks can be deceiving," he told her, still holding tightly to his date's hand. "You're not going to get our picture?" he asked Shane with a smile creeping to his lips. He knew he was messing with her.

"Boy, I'm not taking your picture with another female. Stop," she said boldly.

"Yo, let me go tend to my date. I'ma

catch y'all later, T," Ashton said, dapping up his best friend and rolling his eyes at Shane, who was flirting in his face.

"I'm going to the ladies' room, Ryan. I'll be right back," Ryan's date told him.

"I'll be right here, Kelsey." When she walked away, he turned to Shane. "Why did you do that?"

"What? I didn't do anything." Shane was having more fun at the dance messing with Ashton and Ryan than if she had actually gone to the dance with either of them. Ryan just shook his head at her. He had never met anyone like her before. She was so unpredictable.

When Ryan walked away, Marisa scolded her, "You need to stop picking on Ashton. I know he's a clown most of the time, but he really likes you."

"I was just about to say the same thing about Ryan. I feel sorry for the guy," Brandi told her. "And even worse for Kelsey. That's my girl too."

"They'll be all right. They shouldn't have come with dates."

"Girl, can't nobody wait around for yo' yellow behind," Brandi told her. "What did you expect?"

"You are a trip, Shane Foster. I'm glad we are friends 'cause you really do have problems," Marisa told her.

CHAPTER 9

Shane

Screaming and yelling were not a common thing in the Fosters' home. Most of the time there was peace and harmony. If there was a disagreement between the Fosters, they were usually able to discuss it in a calm manner. But today was different. Shane could hear her mother's voice from upstairs. She opened her bedroom door at the same time as Robin. They looked at each other. Both shrugged their shoulders. Aiden was fast asleep, so the two of them tip-toed to the top of the staircase to eavesdrop.

"Who is she, Brian? When did it happen?"

"It was a long time ago. You'd just had Shane, and—"

"So when I was at home with our newborn, you were with ... what's her name again? How could you, Brian?" They could hear the pain in their mother's voice. She was hurting. "And now she's saying there's a child. Come on! Where was I when all of this was going on? Is it possible that the baby's yours? Tell me the truth."

"Kim, that girl is not my daughter."

"How can you know for sure?"

"I just know. I used protection."

They could hear a slap as it landed on their father's face. Then footsteps as her heels hit the hardwood floors. Her pace was quick and deliberate. "I never thought that I would be having this conversation with you. Brian Foster, former Navy Seal, always controlled, always following the rules! You disgust me!" their mother yelled.

"Kimberly, don't leave!" their father screamed at her as her keys jingled in her hands.

"Oh, I'm leaving before I do or say something that we will both regret."

She slammed the front door so hard that it shook the entire house. Her truck screeched as she backed out of the driveway. She sounded like she was escaping, not just leaving for a while. They could see their father as he looked out the window as her car sped away. When he turned away from the window, his eyes locked on his two daughters, who were still sitting on the top step. They both looked like little girls again, and he was embarrassed by what they had overheard.

The slamming door had woken Aiden, and his cry cut through the silence. The Fosters each needed space to digest what had happened. The air in their house had begun to close in on them, and they all went opposite directions.

Later that evening, Shane and Robin sat together trying to make sense of the conversation they had overheard.

"He said that it was a long time ago," Shane said, taking up for her father.

"Are you serious, Shane? I can't imagine Gavin telling me that he had been cheating on me right after I had Aiden. That's not cool."

"Yeah, well ..." She didn't know what to say. "Do you think Mom will stay with him?"

"I don't know. She hasn't come home yet," Robin said, looking out the window as if that would bring their mother home. "She probably needs time to cool off."

Shane stayed in Robin's room until they heard their mother's truck. "She's here," Robin warned Shane. They were bracing themselves for round two, but they didn't hear a sound. Their parents locked themselves in their bedroom and didn't come out.

Early the next morning, they were called downstairs for a family meeting. "Girls, your father has something he wants to talk to you about."

Brian Foster cleared his throat. This was his toughest audience, and he knew it. He wanted his daughters to respect him. He wanted to be *worthy* of their respect. He wanted to set a good example. "There's going to be an article in the newspaper. It's going to say things about me. Some of them are true, and some of them are not." They could tell he was struggling.

"It's going to be in the newspaper? The *Port City Tribune*?" Shane asked, shocked that their family's business was going to be out there for everyone to see.

"No, it's actually going to appear in the *Messenger* this week, but who knows where it could go after that. The *Port City*

Tribune may pick it up later. They have a tendency to do that."

"Let him finish, Shane. I want to hear what Dad has to say."

He cleared his throat again. "Okay, well, they interviewed a lady who I used to work with. During the interview, this woman claimed that we'd had an affair."

"Did you?" Robin asked abruptly.

"We had a relationship, yes, but it was a long time ago. Your mother and I—"

"And what about this child we heard you and Mom yelling about? Do we have a half-sister, Dad?" Shane asked her father. Everyone was surprised that she was being so blunt.

He felt very uncomfortable talking to his daughters about such a personal matter. He was humiliated and embarrassed. But his daughters were getting older. He had to prepare them for the rumors and the fallout that was sure to come.

He looked at his wife, who had her arms folded, shutting him and his words out. "We're going to have to do a DNA test. She never told me about a baby back then, so I really don't think that the girl is my daughter."

"Wow," Robin said, disgusted. "Everything's different. Everything!"

"You really did this, Daddy? You really cheated on Mom right after she had me?" Shane asked him, crushed.

"I did." His body slumped, and he looked as though he would cry. "Your mother and I ... we have a great relationship. But back then ... I was having a rough time. You'll see what I mean one day. I made a mistake."

"A rough time for *you*? You have no idea what it's like having a baby. I'm sure it was a rough time for her too. I hope that my husband is better than you are. I hope I never have to 'see what you mean,'" Robin snapped.

As much as Mrs. Foster wanted to let the girls badger their father, she knew that she had to step in. "Girls, I made mistakes during that time too. I may not have cheated, but I could have done some things differently."

"You were postpartum, Mom, you'd had a baby. Don't you dare take up for him." Robin's voice was getting louder and louder.

"So we have to be in public and put on a united front, don't we? What are we supposed to say?" Shane asked him, but she didn't really want an answer. "You said that you wouldn't let this election hurt us, Dad. Well, guess what? It's hurting us," she screamed at him as the tears she'd tried to hold back burned her cheeks.

"You hurt me, Dad. *You* did, not the election. You are not the man I thought you were." Robin's words pierced his heart as he sat at the kitchen table.

"Girls, that's enough," their mother told them. "Normally, parents wouldn't have to be so candid about their relationship, but we didn't want you to find out from the newspaper."

"We don't even read the stupid *Messenger*," Robin told them.

"But you know people who do," their father said without looking at his daughters. "And plus, we can put all of this behind us when I win. Surely you both will be happy about that."

"If you win, Dad. We could go through all of this and you could lose. Have you even considered that?" Robin asked. He didn't have an answer for her. "You know, I feel like we already lost, but we lost something worse than this election. We lost our family."

The Fosters were exhausted. It was only ten in the morning, but they were all feeling frazzled and tired. Shane and Robin were both hurt and wanted to spend some time away from home.

They grabbed their keys, their laptops, and Aiden. They went to the one place where they could find some peace: Starbucks. A good coffee drink could make everything a little more bearable.

CHAPTER 10

Marisa

"Marisa Maldonado, please," the unfamiliar voice said.

"This is Marisa."

"This is Stormy calling from Gap. Do you have a minute?"

"Yes, ma'am, I do." Marisa could feel her heart beating rapidly. She sat down on her bed, anxiously waiting for Stormy to respond.

She had already prepared herself to hear the words and had practiced her reaction. *It's okay. I'll just have to try again next time, but thank you so much for considering me.* She didn't want to get her hopes up. She knew that this open call was a shot in the dark.

"Well, I have news for you about the casting call. Are you sitting down?"

Just say it already, she thought.

"Gap has decided to use you in the new fall ad campaign. The shoot will be done in Houston." Marisa began to dance in her room like a maniac. She was quiet enough; Stormy couldn't hear it, but she was dancing. "Will that be a problem?"

"No," she said, trying to catch her breath.

"Are you okay?" Stormy asked, concerned by the change in Marisa's voice.

"Oh, I'm better than okay. I'm elated, excited, and nervous all at the same time."

Stormy laughed. "Well, good. Keep that energy and bring it with you on Monday. And Marisa ... welcome to Gap."

Marisa did laps around the house. She went through the living room where her sisters were watching television, past the kitchen where her mom was making her father's favorite soup, and into Romero's room where he was working hard to beat his best friend Sam on his Xbox. She could hear the concern in their voices as she screamed and yelled as loud as she could.

"I got it. I did it. I got it. I did it," she kept chanting over and over.

They didn't know what she was talking about. "Something's wrong with her," she heard her sisters say.

"Slow down, *mi hija*," her mother's voice faded out as she was on to the next room.

"Something is *so* wrong with your sister, dude," she could hear Samuel warning Romero.

She collapsed on the living room floor. They all gathered to find out what was going on. "I did it. I landed the Gap ad," she said breathlessly.

Her little sisters, Isi and Nadia, began to jump up and down. It took her mom a moment for the news to sink in. They all needed something positive to happen, and this was it. Her mother's hands moved slowly to her mouth as the tears fell from her eyes.

She had always encouraged Marisa in her modeling, but she thought it was an improbable dream. She would have preferred if she'd gone to math or science camp. But she knew that this was a dream come true for her daughter, and she had done it on her own.

Romero explained to Samuel what was going on, and he was thoroughly impressed. "Cool, Mari! Can I get your autograph? I know a real live model."

Marisa was spent from her sprint around the house, but she pulled herself together and called her girls. Once all calls had been joined, she just began to scream. "I got it! I got the Gap ad!" Shane and Brandi shouted congratulations to Marisa. They were excited for their friend.

By the time her dad got home, she had simmered down. She was able to calmly explain what happened and give him all the details. He was concerned about his daughter entering that world at such a young age, but their family needed the extra income, and Marisa swore she would use it to help them get out of the hole they were in.

"I'm proud of you, mi hija," her father told her, kissing her gently on the forehead.

On the Friday before the shoot, Mrs. Maldonado reminded Marisa to pick up her assignments from her teachers for the following Monday.

The Maldonados were determined that Marisa would not get behind in her schoolwork just because she was modeling. Marisa promised them that she would get her schoolwork done.

All weekend long, she prepared for her first photo shoot. She was at the mirror practicing her angles. She drank water constantly so her skin could stay well-hydrated, and she ate fruit to illuminate her natural skin tone. The last thing she wanted was to look dehydrated and malnourished.

Her call time was eight that Monday morning, which meant that she had to be up by five. If the Maldonados could have afforded it, Marisa and her mom would have driven to Houston on Sunday and relaxed in a hotel for the early-morning shoot on Monday. But that was out of the question. Luckily, they wanted her to come with clean hair and face, which meant no makeup or hair care was needed, just wash and go.

As soon as she walked into the studio, she was introduced to the hair and makeup team that would be working with her. They started with hair first. Marisa was instructed to come to the shoot with freshly washed hair that had no product added after washing. The hair team spritzed her hair with water, then gave her a blowout. Next came oversized rollers, which set while her makeup was applied.

The makeup artist was a twentyish Asian girl with numerous tattoos. She had a few strategically placed piercings that Marisa thought were really cool. Marisa realized she was a little intimidated by this interesting young woman. She seemed unapproachable, so Marisa just sat quietly until the makeup artist broke the silence.

"Is this your first shoot?" she asked.

Marisa looked up. After what seemed like thirty minutes of silence, she was caught off guard. "Yes," she said shyly. "Can you tell?"

The makeup artist laughed. "Yeah, but it's cool. We all start somewhere. I'm Alexis."

"I'm Marisa, but call me Mari."

"Well, Mari, I think that you'll do just

fine. You have a good look, and I've seen a lot of looks."

"Thanks," Marisa told her and went back to studying the assignment for her English class. The vocabulary words that she had to learn seemed to be the easiest thing to study while having to meet Alexis's demands.

"Close your eyes. Tilt your head. Look to the right."

Marisa was constantly losing her focus. What made her think she could concentrate when everyone around her was so busy? Not only that, she was ordered to tilt her head up, down, right, and left every few minutes.

She had never understood how long it took to properly apply makeup for a photo shoot. She gasped when Alexis pulled out an airbrush.

"Hey," Alexis said. "Don't be nervous. This is a really cool tool. All your photos will be indoors, so I don't want you to look washed out. Your skin will be a touch darker than you're used to. But don't freak out. The photos will be fab."

"I never thought I'd need ... is something wrong with me?" Marisa asked nervously.

"Heck no! You are gorgeous. This will just apply a fine mist of makeup. The flash won't bounce the light off your skin. And if you get hot? The color won't change. My work never smudges," Alexis said proudly.

"Who knew?" Mari smiled. "This is beyond sweet!"

And with that, Marisa decided to put her schoolwork aside. There was no way she could pull off the photo shoot that would launch her career *and* do her English assignment at the same time.

Her hair was styled by a guy named Marco, who seemed to know how to work magic. She had never seen her hair look this good. He was pleased that she was pleased. It had taken three hours to do hair and makeup alone.

By the time she arrived at wardrobe, she felt like she needed a nap. She was waiting patiently when her mother showed up, asking if she had eaten anything. She hadn't even thought of food in the past three hours. She was more focused on completing the shoot and living up to expectations.

She declined her mother's offer to eat and went into wardrobe, where they fussed over the perfect look for the shot. In the end, she wore a pair of jeans that tightly hugged her body, a plaid shirt, brown boots, and a stylish scarf.

It was amazing. There were so many people running around trying to perfect this shoot. But Marisa felt like a bystander until she got in front of the camera and realized that all this fuss was for her. She was the star of the day, and it felt like it. The experience was surreal.

As the photographer gave her directions, she did her best to give him what she thought he was looking for. "Wonderful, don't lose your neck. Extend, extend. Throw the leaves into the air. Look toward the light. Look happy. Good, good." She felt like a contortionist. "Now let's take a break," he said after an hour of shooting.

"You did great, mi hija," her mother said, handing her a bottle of water.

When she returned to the set, there was a young male model there to shoot with her. He was possibly the cutest white boy Marisa had ever laid eyes on. His etched face gave him a superhero appearance. He was absolutely gorgeous.

Marisa could feel her heart thumping as he introduced himself. His wardrobe mirrored hers. The navy blue sweater he wore picked up the colors in her flannel. They added a navy blue infinity scarf to Marisa's wardrobe plus a cute hat with a flower. The two made an adorable couple.

"Here we go, people!" the photographer's assistant yelled.

The sound of the fan whirling, let the models know that it was game on. The scene was set for them. "It's a regular autumn day. The leaves have begun to fall. It's breezy. The two of you are strolling through the park. You stop to take in the moment and enjoy a quiet Sunday afternoon together. Whatever you do, don't forget you're here for the clothing. Let's go."

Marisa's partner turned it up. As he posed, she slinked into the crevasses of his body. They looked as though they were having fun. They looked like a real couple who just fit. The laughter they shared was realistic. He was a cool kid. He picked up the leaves from the ground and playfully let them fall like rain on her head. She smiled up at him as the leaves danced in the air. The shoot was magical. They were young and fresh, just what the photographer said Gap was looking for.

When they finished that portion of the shoot, Marisa was approached by one of the ladies who had been observing them. "Hey, that was great. I really enjoyed watching your shoot today."

"Oh, thanks," Marisa said, appreciating the compliment, but exhausted from the long day. It was already four in the afternoon, and they still had to drive all the way back to Port City.

Her mother had already started gathering their things.

"I'm Marcie Miller," she said, handing Marisa her business card, which read Miller & Miller Modeling Inc. "I wanted to talk to you about representation. At Miller and Miller, we are always looking for fresh faces, and you definitely have that. Do you already have an agent?"

Marisa had never thought about having an agent. She was just reacting to what was going on around her. Her plan had only gone as far as beating out the competition at the casting call and booking the job.

Her mother was just a couple of steps away, listening to the whole conversation. She stepped in just in time. "I'm Marisa's mother, Lupe. Do you mind if I have one of your cards? We can give you a call later this week."

Marisa was so thankful that her mother was able to speak English with confidence. She couldn't imagine if she had to navigate through this new world of modeling alone.

"That's a wonderful idea," Marcie said. "Just know that what I saw today shows some really raw talent. I believe that Marisa can go far. Why don't you do some research on our agency and then give me a call." She turned to Marisa. "It was nice to meet you. We look forward to working with you."

After Marcie left the Maldonados alone, her mother turned to her with tears in her eyes. "You made me so proud today, mi hija. And now we can check out this agent and see if she's any good. I know your father wants to know all the details. I can't wait to tell him. This is such a wonderful opportunity for you, but I want you to remember, school comes first." She looked stern. "If your grades drop, no more modeling until you can prove you can handle it."

Marisa knew her mother was right. She would do her best with her grades. But what she was really fixated on was her glamorous new career. She felt like her life was just beginning. Maybe she would make it to Paris and Milan someday. She felt like her life was just beginning.

CHAPTER 11

Brandi

"Get dressed," Brandi's mother said, pulling the covers off her daughter. "It's almost eleven."

"Whaaat, Mom? It's spring break! All I want to do is sleep these ten days away."

"Negative. Raven," her mother yelled. "We have good news for you girls. We are going to that new restaurant For Starters to celebrate because Daddy got a job yesterday at the plant."

"What? Are you serious?" Brandi asked, excited for her father.

Raven started singing and dancing.

"New clothes, new clothes. Mama, can I get the new pink Js?" she asked.

"Can you stop spending your father's checks before he gets them?" her mother asked playfully.

"Mom, that's cool and all, but I was going to meet up with Bryce this afternoon. Is it okay if he joins us?"

Her mom was skeptical about her relationship with Bryce, and Brandi knew it. "Well, this is more for family, B," she said. "But I guess it's okay." She wanted them to be in a celebratory mood, which meant that she would have to put up with Bryce.

"Cool, Mom!" Brandi said excitedly. "Thank you, thank you, thank you. I'm going to call Bryce."

After Brandi called Bryce, she left to get ready for their afternoon lunch. It was the first time that her family was going to spend time with him in an intimate setting. She just prayed they would warm up to him, even while that voice in her head told her to back off. There had been red flags all over the place, but Brandi was hoping she was wrong. Maybe Bryce could pull it together.

In the car, Brandi could hear her parents discussing an article that had appeared in the newspaper; she knew it had to be about Mr. Foster.

"I just can't believe Brian is the cheating type. He's so buttoned-up," her mother said.

"I just hope that the child is not his. I'm thinking Kim would leave my boy if that was the case. You see, baby, every-body makes mistakes. At least you don't have to worry about me cheating on you," her father responded.

"I better not. We already have too much going on as it is."

They pulled up to Bryce's house to pick him up. It was a modest home that he shared with his grandmother, who waved at them from the porch.

"Go in the house, Momo," he yelled at her. He seemed to be in an awful mood. It was in obvious contrast to the playful, upbeat vibe that was going on in the Haywoods' car.

"How are you, Bryce?" Mrs. Haywood asked.

"I'm good. Thanks for letting me roll with y'all."

"Thanks for rolling with us," her father said, noticing how rough Bryce was around the edges. He was not the kind of boy he wanted his daughter dating. He was bettering himself so that his daughters would make better choices. And Bryce had an air of defiance and smugness about him that didn't sit well with Mr. Haywood.

He knew he hadn't been the best role model for his oldest daughter. But he hadn't realized until his last stint in rehab how much his choices influenced her actions. While Bryce was not like him, he was truly a damaged boy. And he did not want his daughters ending up with men who could harm them emotionally or physically. Men like him.

Bryce sat back listening to the family interaction. When he first met Brandi, their lives seemed similar. Even more so when they started dating. Both of their parents were battling drug addiction. Brandi basically had no father. Now it had all changed for her, and he was feeling alone. He scrolled through his phone and noticed that Matthew Kincade, Brandi's ex-boyfriend, had posted on her Friender timeline.

"What's this?" he asked, showing Brandi the Friender page on his phone.

"I guess that's a post on my timeline. What?" she whispered so that her parents wouldn't hear them.

"What's Matthew doing asking you what's up?" he hissed.

"You two okay back there?" her mother asked.

"Yeah, we good," he said and turned to look out the window.

When they arrived at the restaurant, Bryce looked at the sign: For Starters, A Tapas Experience. "What's *tapas*?" Bryce asked, his face contorting like there was a foul odor in the air.

"It's when a restaurant focuses on appetizers instead of large meals," Mrs. Haywood explained. "It's one way of tasting a variety of food in one place. It's new, so we thought we'd try it."

"Well, I don't think I'm going to like it."

"There's a McDonald's down the street if that's better for you," Mr. Haywood told him, annoyed by his negativity. There was no way he was about to let this angry little punk ruin their mood. Bryce shot him a look like he was tempted to say something smart, but by the expression on Mr. Haywood's face, he thought better of it.

"I'm good," he replied, cowering under Mr. Haywood's gaze.

The rest of the time at the restaurant, the Haywoods tried to ignore Bryce and his negative comments. He was a hurt little kid with a chip on his shoulder, which was a horrible combination.

They dined on tuna tartar, fried macaroni and cheese, boudin balls, crab-stuffed peppers, and jalapeño poppers. The fresh strawberry lemonade really quenched their thirst. The Haywood family hadn't had an afternoon lunch that tasted this good in a long time. After Bryce tasted the food at For Starters, his attitude even began to improve. A little.

As soon as they left the restaurant, they headed to the park to feed the ducks and enjoy the beautiful spring day.

Mr. Haywood took Raven to the swings and gave her a push to get her going. Then he stood back and watched her happy face.

Their mother sat down on one of the benches. It was a joy for her to be watching her family having a good time. As Brandi and Bryce strolled around the duck pond, Bryce's attitude suddenly shifted.

"What's wrong?" Brandi asked. When he didn't respond, she followed his gaze. She saw Matthew Kincade coming their way.

"Hey, B! What are y'all doing here? I just now noticed your moms over there on the bench."

"Hey, Mattie," she said nervously, knowing Bryce was probably still mad about the Friender post. "Did Dad see you? He just asked about you the other day."

"Aw, man. I didn't know that your dad was back in town. That's great! Where's Raven?

"Um, I hate to break up y'all's little reunion, but I ain't havin' none of this. You just gonna disrespect me like I ain't even standin' here?"

Brandi had seen this change in Bryce's personality before, and she knew that he was about to get irate. Again the red-flag alert went off in her head. Trying to avoid a scene, she said, "Baby, I'm sorry. I wasn't trying to disrespect you." She looked at Matthew apologetically with her eyes.

"Man, you ain't 'bout to sit here talking to me like I'm a chump or somethin'," Bryce hissed between clenched teeth. "I can see what's goin' on here, and I'm not down with it at all."

Brandi was losing her patience and becoming more embarrassed. "You trippin', Bryce. You supposed to know I'm your ride or die, but you treating me like I'm out here running around on you just because I spoke to Matthew. Of course he knows my family. We were together for two years."

"Man, forget this," Bryce said, pushing Brandi. She lost her balance and fell to the ground. When her father saw her fall, he ran from the playground area toward Bryce. Before he could get there, Matthew was in Bryce's face.

"Man, what's wrong with you? Don't you know everything she's been through? Now here you come, making her situation worse."

"Dog, you better back up off me!" Bryce yelled at him.

"Nah, you wanna put your hands on her. Put your hands on me, pretty boy." Matthew jumped at him like he was going to slap him in the face. Bryce flinched. "That's what I thought. You a scared li'l punk."

"I ain't scared of nobody," Bryce said, taking his jacket off. Before the jacket hit the ground, Matthew punched him in the nose, sending blood flying through the air.

"Mattie!" Brandi yelled. "Don't," she begged him. She knew that Matthew would hurt Bryce. Even though he had pushed her, she didn't want it to get violent.

"I'm sorry, B. I was just trying to speak to you and the fam."

Mr. Haywood, who had been standing by and keeping an eye on the boys, said, "No need to apologize. Looks to me like he had it coming."

This made Bryce even angrier. "Man, I'm outta here," he said, walking away from the group. "Brandi, we are done," he shouted back at her.

"Tilt that head back. The bleeding will stop," Matthew said, making fun of Bryce.

Brandi would always have a place in Matthew's heart. She had been his girlfriend through middle school. After she was abducted the previous school year, he swore in his heart that he would look out for her.

He had to make it up to her because he had ruined their relationship by cheating on her. And he didn't do much better freshman year when he tried to date Marisa. She had forgiven him for a lot.

The Haywoods all thanked Matthew, who felt like a hero.

"It was nothing. I'm just glad I could help," Matthew said bashfully.

By the time that drama was over, they were ready to leave. "Mom, can I talk to Matt for a second?"

"Sure, baby. We'll be in the car. And, Matthew," Mrs. Haywood said, "thanks again."

Brandi turned to Matthew when her parents were out of listening range. "You really didn't have to do that."

"You mad at me?"

"Of course not. Bryce is a jerk. I was kind of trying to get rid of him. He was great one minute, awful the next. You know I'm bad with good-bye, though. You saw how long it took me to break up with your cheating behind," she snickered.

"Aw, I wasn't that bad," he said. She looked at him doubtfully. "Okay, maybe I was," he agreed.

"And you still are, but you know I love you, right?" He shook his head and looked down. She tilted his chin so she could look in his eyes. "Always will," she said. "Always will," she said, giving him a kiss on the cheek. "Hey, I gotta go. You know Raven is gonna be talking about you all day. She misses you."

"I miss all of you. Especially you, B. I wish ... I wish I—

"Matt, don't go there. We are much better as friends."

"I know. I know. Just take care of yourself so I won't have to make nobody else bleed."

"Fair enough," she said, laughing as she headed off to the car.

CHAPTER 12

The Fundraiser

*J*oin us at five as Fox News reporter Macey McMillan sits down with the former mistress of Area Fourteen council member hopeful Brian Foster. It's a must-see interview," the reporter announced from the TV screen. Mrs. Foster had a look of irritation and distaste as she passed by the television. She grabbed the remote and clicked it off.

"I don't want to hear that garbage," she told her daughters. "And you shouldn't want to either."

"Well, I want to know what that

hoochie is saying about Dad," Shane said. "And you two are acting like she's just going to go away. She's *not* just going to go away.

"And what about the girl? I looked up her Friender page. She's cute, but she better not be my sister. Her mama need to go on one of those talk shows and find her real baby daddy," Shane continued, disgusted by this woman tainting her father's name.

"I can't believe that she's doing interviews," Robin, who was equally outraged, added.

"Nobody outside of Port City is watching her. She's getting like five minutes of fame instead of fifteen. I'm not worrying about that opportunist. You hear about women coming forward all the time, telling all of their business for some camera time, and then you never hear about them again. I'm sure the same thing will happen with that woman too, and we can go back to our normal, boring life."

"You sure are taking this well," Robin said, suspicious of her mother's behavior.

"Don't think I'm not furious with your father. Because I am. We're going to be working on trust for quite some time. But you don't just throw it all away. At least I don't," Mrs. Foster said.

"Besides, we want to stay married. And you can't do that if you hold a grudge. My grandmother used to tell me that. Funny, but I never knew what she meant until now."

This was not a topic Mrs. Foster wanted to continue. "Enough of this," she declared. "I'm going to need you girls to help out at the fundraiser tomorrow. Robin, can Gavin watch Aiden?"

"No, Gavin's going to help too. His mom said she would watch Aiden."

"Okay, well, Mrs. Maldonado has her team ready to go. Are Marisa and Brandi going to be there?"

"Mom, you know they are."

"I have some of my girls from the college who are coming out to help too," Robin told her.

"I am so ready to get tomorrow over with. That woman's accusations are making us work a lot harder for campaign contributions. Until the DNA test results come back and are revealed, it's just words. I guess people don't know what to believe; they sure aren't sending checks anymore, I know that.

"We need more radio ads and bill-boards. Stringer's face is all over Port City. We have to get your dad more exposure. This fundraiser has to be a success. So much to do, so little time." Their mother went upstairs to continue planning for the next day. She still had a lot to do for the fundraiser.

"You did tape that lady's interview, right?" Shane asked her sister.

"You know I did." Robin laughed. "You

and I are not about to be caught walking around clueless while people are laughing at us."

The next day they were at the park bright and early setting up for the fundraiser. They placed a banner at the entrance to the park that had a large picture of Mr. Foster on it. The banner read, "When you want honest and fair, Brian Foster will be there."

Because of the wording of the campaign slogan, his opponent jumped on the opportunity to point out that his dishonesty in his marriage would carry over into his work. "If his wife can't trust him, how can the citizens of Port City!" he shouted to his supporters during his rallies. The infidelity issue had taken on a life of its own.

The campaign needed more money, which it had been bleeding since the negative ads began. Hopefully the fundraiser would be successful. There were bounce houses for the kids and food carts everywhere.

The Maldonados were in one booth selling tamales and tacos with homemade guacamole, salsa, and tortillas. The Haywoods were in another booth selling smoked boudin, turkey legs, and links on a bun. The Foster family was focused on interacting with as many people in the community as possible.

Halfway through the event, they ran out of food and had to resupply their carts. It seemed like the whole community was there cheering on Mr. Foster. The negative press had been so hateful that after momentarily questioning his integrity, the voters returned to support him in full force.

The girls decided to meet up at four to finally take a much-needed break. They had been pulled in every direction all day and knew that the cleanup was going to be a beast. A break just before cleanup was the best time to sneak off for some girl time.

"See, I wouldn't mind hitting a blunt right now," Shane said, relaxing her feet after being on them all day. "I'm exhausted, and this drama with my dad and the other woman is stressing me out."

"I *wish* I would see a blunt in your hand after what we went through with your high yellow behind last year," Brandi warned her.

"For reals," Marisa said, agreeing with her. "Don't even play like that."

"It was a joke. Ha-ha. You know you two should lighten up some. I can't get down like that anymore. Daddy would kill me. It would be on the front page of the *Messenger* tomorrow," she laughed.

"Still not funny," Brandi told her. "What if I was joking about some guy I was dating that I met on the Internet? Would you find it funny?"

"Touché," Shane responded. "So, did y'all have fun today?" She was hoping her family hadn't worked her friends too hard.

"Girl, I had a *good* time! Oh, except when Bryce's creepy self came by." Brandi made a face. "Seriously, I can't be with that dude anymore," she said. "Plus, I can tell he's super angry since Matt put him in his place the other day."

"That story was hilarious. Go, Mattie!" Marisa cheered him on. She turned her attention back to Shane, "Seriously, everybody was here supporting your dad: Mrs. Monroe, Ashton, Trent, the principal ..."

"Ryan stopped by to see me, and Riley came too. I guess that's why I was talking about weed. She's a trigger for me. Remember, she was my li'l smoking buddy back in the gap."

"Shane, shut it!" Brandi spat, slugging her friend good. She was tired of hearing about the good ole days with Riley. They were the ones picking her up when Riley was helping her fall.

"I can't believe that Brendon Cooper came. Y'all remember that guy who dropped my butt on the side of the road. I didn't even wanna speak to him and his li'l crew. He's lucky I was selling links for your dad so I couldn't go ham on him."

"I was happy to see Hayley and Christina. Even Ashley came by to get tacos. I'm telling you, everyone in Port City was here. I think your dad's got this in the bag. Councilman Stringer better look out," Marisa announced. "Hey, let's go get this park cleaned up. I see Mama looking for me."

"Where are all those people we named? We should have recruited some help," Brandi announced.

"We'll be done in no time," Marisa told them. "Come on, let's get it over with."

What would I do without my girls? Shane thought. *I'm so lucky to have them.*

CHAPTER 13

Shane

$\mathcal{M}$r. Foster's city council campaign seemed to be making time fly. Every day the family had to participate in some event—sometimes there was more than one! Most days, as soon as Shane got home from school, she was picking out clothing to go to a party, a fundraiser, a press conference, or a photo opportunity. That was only the tip of the iceberg for the Foster family.

Tonight was no different. They were invited to yet another event. This one was taking place at God's People Church. They weren't members of the church, but Shane had visited there a few times. Tonight's event showcased up-and-coming gospel artists in the area. Mr. Foster thought that it would be a good opportunity for the family to go out and mingle with more people.

"I don't understand why you have to drag us to all of these stupid events. Robin and I aren't running for anything. You and Mom can go alone. It's Friday night, and I don't want to spend it with a whole bunch of church people I don't know."

"You better stop complaining and get dressed. I really don't feel like hearing any drama, Shane," her father warned.

"Hey, why don't you and Robin go to the mall and get something to wear," her mother suggested. "Just take Daddy's card. I'll watch Aiden."

"See? Mom speaks my language."

"It's my money she's offering up. I don't get any credit?" He sounded stern, but her dad was smiling as he said it.

"Nope," Shane said, kissing her mom on the cheek and running to tell Robin.

It took forever for her sister to get ready. First Aiden started to cry, then she had to get his bottles ready, and then she wanted to make sure that there were enough diapers.

"Come on," Shane complained after waiting for twenty minutes.

"Girl, I have to make sure my little man is good before I leave. You'll understand one day."

They hit the mall armed and ready with their dad's plastic. First it was Gap, American Eagle, and Forever 21. Then on to T.J. Maxx for some real bargains. They were sure they'd maxed out their father's credit card. They'd even done some damage at the makeup counter.

By the time they'd left, they had purchased outfits for the night's event and entire new spring wardrobes. Good-bye to those dark winter colors, and hello to the coral, orange, sage, and white hues of a lovely Texas spring.

They even went a little crazy shopping for baby boy clothes. Aiden totally scored, not that he would ever know. They'd grabbed a few polo shirts, plaid shorts, and tiny topsiders for him.

They looked at each other on the ride home and giggled nervously. It felt good to get back at their father just a little bit. A little devilish. He deserved a little pain in the wallet.

Both Shane and Robin looked great in the new outfits they had purchased for the God's People event that evening. They were both ready for spring.

By the time the whole family was dressed and ready to go, the event had been going on for thirty minutes. "We are late. I hate being late," her mother complained.

"Mom, I don't just have to get myself ready. I have to think about Aiden too."

"I know, baby, but that means you need to start earlier."

"Or you need to help more."

"Here we go with that again—"

"Hey, Foster women, chill out. I have enough on my mind right now. I don't need upheaval in my home too," Mr. Foster interrupted.

When they arrived, they were ushered to a table that had been designated for their family. Many of the other people running for city council had already arrived. The Foster family took their seats and sat back to enjoy the music.

The food was being served simultaneously with the performances. Dinner and gospel music—it mixed well. When Shane got up to refill their drinks, she was surprised to see Ryan Petry there. "What are you doing here?"

"This is my church. What are you doing here?" he asked.

"Gotta support the fam. You don't

strike me as the churchgoing type, I have to say."

"Well, you don't either," he said matter-of-factly.

"Well, I am. Hey, let me drop these drinks off at our table, and then we can catch up."

Shane and Ryan stepped outside to talk. She enjoyed his company. The air between them was so easy at times, but he was leaving in just four months for college. Shane was no fool. She wasn't about to get involved with a senior and set herself up for heartbreak.

"When are you going to let me take you out again?" he asked.

"I'm not."

"Why? I know you want to."

"You're leaving for college, Ryan. I'm sure you'll meet a lot of girls like me, beautiful, smart, cool ... well, maybe not."

"Definitely not," he said, moving closer to her.

Shane could feel her heart beating. The closer he came, the harder it was to breathe. When someone burst through of the door, it startled the two of them. It was her father.

"You swore you would keep them out of this. I will not have my girls ridiculed. They're going through enough as it is with the Sasha situation. You fix this or else I'm out of this race!" he screamed into the phone.

He turned to go back into the building, but Shane stopped him. "Dad?"

"Oh, Shane, what are you doing out here? Hi, Ryan," he said, shaking Ryan's hand and trying to calm himself down.

"What was that about, Dad?" she asked.

"Nothing, baby, nothing for you to worry about."

Shane was nervous. She heard what her father had said, but she didn't want to press him. It wasn't the time or the place, and she knew it. They all went back inside together.

"Pick up where we left off later?" Ryan whispered to her as his lips grazed the back of her neck.

Chills ran down her spine, and she tingled all over. The butterflies in her stomach started to dance. She had to run from him. The last thing she expected was to find herself attracted to Ryan Petry. This had come out of nowhere, and she wanted it to stop.

She took her seat next to Robin and grabbed Aiden, who was squirming all over the place. The loud music was interrupting what would have been his bedtime.

Robin went on a much-needed restroom break. Shane was not surprised that her mother hadn't taken Aiden from Robin. She talked a good game about helping them more, but it just wasn't who she was. She was getting better, but she still had a way to go.

When they got into the car, no one uttered a word. Shane wanted to know what her father was talking about on the phone, but he wasn't saying anything, and Shane was a little afraid to bring it up. She didn't know what to do.

Her mother could sense that something was wrong. She reached out to touch her husband's hand. "Is everything okay?"

"Yeah, I just have a lot on my mind," he told her.

"Maybe it's what you were yelling about on your phone," Shane mumbled.

"Let it go, Shane," he said. Then his phone started ringing. He quickly picked it up. "That's not okay. ... And we can't do anything about it? ... Well, I'm not running anymore. ... This is over, Clyde. I'm done. ... No, I won't think about this," he said, hanging up the phone abruptly.

"What, Brian? What happened now?" Mrs. Foster pushed.

"Not now," he whispered to his wife.

He turned his face away. But then Mr. Foster took a deep breath, turned back toward his family, and began to speak. He had some devastating news to share with them. "There's another article being posted in the *Messenger* tomorrow."

"What did you do now?" Mrs. Foster asked him automatically, taking her hand away from his.

"Nothing, it's, um ..." he hesitated, "it's about the girls."

"What?!" Robin shouted.

"There's going to be an article in the *Messenger* tomorrow. They found out about Shane's brief visit to rehab last year, and they are going to write about it. Robin, they have you painted in a negative light because of Aiden."

"Dad, you have to do something," Shane demanded.

"I can't stop them from running the article. I've already tried. The owner of the *Messenger* is good friends with Stringer.

It's all politics, baby girl. My hands are tied. Even if I drop out of the race, it's too late. They are definitely printing the article."

When they pulled up at the house, it was mayhem. They were all angry and taking it out on each other.

Robin and Shane were mortified that their lives were about to be on display for all of Port City to see. They took their frustrations out on their father, even though they knew if he could have sheltered them from this humiliation, he would have. There was nothing they could do but wait for the paper to come out in the morning. No amount of yelling could stop the inevitable.

The next day, Mr. Foster was up bright and early to go to the corner store to purchase four copies of the *Messenger*. But when he opened the front door, there were ten copies on their front porch. He could see the family picture they had taken at Christmas right in the middle of the page.

His heart dropped as he bent down to pick up the papers. He looked around to see if the person who left them was still around, but there was no movement on the street.

He sat alone in his office to read the article. It made him sick. The article concluded, "How can he lead a city when his home is this dysfunctional?"

They painted a picture of Shane as a pot-smoking, pill-popping sophomore who could not be controlled. Robin was portrayed as a promiscuous teenager, who once showed great promise but threw it all away to chase after boys.

Mr. Foster knew that his daughters were going to be hurt and embarrassed—and angry. He felt that it was his fault, and he had to figure out a way to soften the blows.

"Clyde, it's me. Did you read the article yet? ... Well, as my campaign manager, I would think you would have been up at the crack of dawn trying to get a copy too. ... No, Clyde, I'm not going to ignore it. It's not about me, it's about my girls. ... You know what, you're fired. I'm going to handle my own PR." Mr. Foster was livid. He wanted to blame somebody. He knew it wasn't Clyde's fault, but he was angry.

Mr. Foster sat back to reflect on what had taken place. He had to show the girls the article. It was time for another family meeting.

As they all gathered around the breakfast table, their father handed each of them their own copy of the paper. He could see the shock on their faces as they read the article detailing their lives. He had to keep his composure. They had to believe he had all of this under control.

"This is a joke, right?" Robin asked in disbelief. Mr. Foster shook his head. "I can't believe that this is in the paper. I sound like a slut." She read it again. "I am not promiscuous. I've been with Gavin forever. We plan on getting married and everything. I'm suing the *Messenger*!" Robin was livid.

Shane sat there sipping hot chocolate. Her blank stare alarmed her parents. "Shane!" her mother yelled. "Snap out of it."

"I can't blame anyone but myself," she said calmly, not wanting to meet her father's gaze. Tears welled up in her eyes. "I know that my behavior has hurt you, and I'm sorry." The tears she was trying to fight began to fall down her cheeks. It was a much different reaction than her father had anticipated.

"Don't feel bad, baby. This family has borne the brunt of all of the negative press that's been thrown our way, but we are tough. How about we fight back?" he asked, more hopeful than ever before.

"Now, you're speaking my language," Mrs. Foster said, ready to fight for her family. "Nobody talks about my babies like that!"

Mr. Foster called a press conference at City Hall that same day.

They were all there, including Aiden and Gavin. Mr. Foster had called all of the major news outlets to come. "My opponent, Mr. Stringer, would have you think that all families are perfect, but they aren't, and neither is his. But I am *not* going to stoop to his level and put all of his dirty laundry on the front page of the newspaper. Instead, I want to reintroduce you to my family."

He pointed out each of them and said their names. "We are broken, yet fixable. We have all made mistakes, but still we stand. Our family is much like Port City, perfect and flawed at the same time. If you look at my girls, you see beauty and hope in their eyes, even though we have made mistakes.

"That is what the Foster family will bring back to this town, the ability to see a mistake and make it right, and not just gloss over the problem. Mr. Stringer believes in glossing over problems in his family and his city. I believe in facing them head-on, which is why I had the DNA test."

There was a hush in the crowd. "And the results are in. That little girl is one hundred percent not my child. I feel sorry for her. Her mother and Mr. Stringer used her as a pawn in their little game.

"That mean-spirited behavior is what Stringer is known for. He doesn't care who gets hurt as long as he gets what he wants. He believes what he's doing works for this city, and I'm here to tell you that it doesn't.

"I want to show you what a councilman who cares about your city can do. I will work until Port City is a replica of the one that I called home many years ago." Mr. Foster paused. "Mr. Stringer, this message is for you," he said, pointing to the cameras. "If you think dragging my family through the mud will deter me from helping this city, then you have another thing coming." The crowd went wild. As they cheered, he concluded, "Brian Foster, Area Fourteen ... get out and vote! Thank you for coming out."

Those who supported the Foster family cheered excitedly. The news reporters began to pan the crowd for live shots to add to the evening news. When it aired on the news stations, all of the wonderful things that Mr. Foster said were taken out. The only thing left was the message to Mr. Stringer, who refused to comment.

In the *Port City Tribune*, Mr. Foster's speech was very detailed and well-documented. The newspaper didn't just have sound bites, it had it all. Their family had been vindicated that day, and the Foster name was intact. With very few days left until voting day, the campaign was stronger than ever.

CHAPTER 14

Marisa

The Maldonados were a family in transition. Mr. Maldonado was having a hard time recovering from the time he spent in jail because of his courtroom outbursts—which had almost got him deported as well.

Making matters worse, the family was experiencing a financial crunch. Mr. Maldonado had always been the family's primary breadwinner, but his once lucrative construction business was bleeding money because he had been away for too long.

While he was in jail, there was no one to generate new business or give estimates to potential customers. And the customers he did have weren't completely happy with the service they received while Mr. Maldonado was away.

When he was released from custody, he discovered that some of his customers had moved on to other companies. So months later, Mr. Maldonado found himself doing what he could to rebuild his business—and his reputation.

Luckily, Marisa's modeling career had taken off since her first shoot with Gap. Not only had Gap asked her to do another campaign for their multicultural ads, but her new agent, Marcie Miller, was putting her to work. Marcie had approached her during that first shoot and their relationship took off. She proved that she believed in Marisa.

After her Gap shoot, she had been booked for a Ford Focus ad. When the local advertisers in Houston were sent her photos and cover letter, she got their attention. She was a fresh face who they felt would appeal to the growing Hispanic community. She had only been modeling for a little over a month, but people were starting to know who she was.

The morning of her third shoot in Houston was a struggle for Marisa. She gathered the items she needed, her backpack, water bottle, pillow and blanket for the car, and her tablet to read the novel she had downloaded. It was still four in the morning, and they had a long ride ahead.

"Let's go, mi hija. You are going to be late," her mom said, like she had already been up for hours.

"Mom, it's four in the morning. How can anybody be late if they are ready to go at four. We will be okay."

"Your call time is at six. It takes two hours to get to Houston. You do the math."

Marisa rolled her eyes. She knew she

shouldn't be mean to her mother. Mrs. Maldonado was rearranging her schedule to be the chauffeur. She realized how important modeling was to her daughter.

Marisa was tired and grumpy, but she knew she could catch some z's in the car. No way could she go on set with dark circles under her eyes. So she tried to make the best of the situation. Everyone was counting on her.

Armed with a water bottle at all times, Marisa took a big gulp. When she drank a lot of water, her skin seems to glow, and that hydration translated in her photographs. She seemed to explode off the page.

Everything mattered now. She was supporting her family. Modeling seemed to be a full-time job.

She slept all the way to Houston. When she arrived on set, they were ready for her in hair and makeup. She tried to do her homework so she would be prepared for school the next day, but it was hard. The stylists were constantly asking her to turn her head, look this way, close her eyes. She gave up on her assignments and focused on the shoot.

She couldn't get her Monday night homework done, but she knew if she could nail the photo shoot, then her career would move even further ahead. Her agent called when she was done to let her know how happy the Ford reps were with the pictures. They wanted to work with her again. Marisa was ecstatic.

"Did you get your homework done?" her mother asked when they were on I-10.

"I tried, Mama, but it was too much."

"Well, take your books out and start now."

"I'm too tired now. I can't focus on Shakespeare or numbers, forget about it."

"Marisa, your father and I only agreed

to this because you said that you would keep up with your schoolwork. So make sure you do that. Now get some rest on the drive home so you can get your work done later."

Marisa reclined her seat and dozed off. Modeling was physically and mentally draining. She had always known it was hard work, and she enjoyed every minute, but she never knew how much it would exhaust her.

When she got back, it was still early. They finished shooting by one o'clock, and they were back in Port City by three. Marisa was missing her friends, so she decided to get dropped off at PCH instead of going home.

"Being at the school will help me focus. I'm going straight to the library," she promised, jumping out of the car. She got to the school when the last bell was about to ring. She went to Shane's locker to wait for her two best friends.

"Mari!" Shane shouted when she saw her. "You're here. How was work?"

"Good and tiring, but I slept in the car."

"America's Next Top Model decided to pay us common folk a visit," Brandi teased her when she got to the lockers.

"You and your jokes," Marisa retorted, turning her mouth up with a small smirk. "Y'all seen Trent anywhere? I'm missing him too."

Out of nowhere Trent appeared in the hallway. He had four freshman cheerleaders smiling up at him like he was a god or something. They were hanging on his every word, and he looked to be enjoying the attention.

"Baby in the building," he said as soon as he laid eyes on Marisa. He grabbed her and hugged her tightly. "How was work, Mari? You came back early to see me?"

"Yeah," she said stiffly.

"What's wrong?" She didn't answer. He turned to Brandi and Shane. "What's up with your girl? Why she giving me the cold shoulder?" They both shrugged, trying to stay out of their drama. They loved Trent, but their loyalties were always with their girl.

"Who are they?" she asked, pointing to the four cheerleaders standing behind Trent.

"Oh, they are my locker girls for basketball season."

"Four locker girls, Trent, really?"

"Brandi should be your locker girl, not them."

Brandi leaned in to Marisa, "Um, not going to happen. I'm not catering to my best friend's man. There's something just wrong with that."

"Well, I don't like it."

"Don't make a scene. Let's just talk later," he whispered.

Brandi looked at the freshmen who had been assigned to Trent and motioned for them to move along.

"Whatever," their leader said, mouthing off. "Bye, Trent. We'll talk later."

"Bye, Trent," the other three said in unison.

"Bye, ladies," he said, smiling and making the girls giggle. Marisa wanted to control herself in front of them, but she punched him in the arm as his gaze fell to their backsides when they walked away.

"You make me sick," she told him, disgusted.

"Girl, I'm a man. I can look, but I promise I won't touch."

"Um-hm, tell me anything. I'm breaking up with you when you go to college. Keep it up."

"Girl, you gonna marry me," he said, picking her up and cradling her in his huge arms. "You think I'm crazy enough to let you go. I'm poppin' bottles with models."

"Boy put me down before you drop me," she demanded.

They heard someone clear their throat

behind them, it was the principal, Mrs. Montgomery. "That's enough, you two. Marisa, were you even in school today?"

"No, ma'am," she said, embarrassed that Trent still had her off her feet. She was talking to Principal Montgomery from the sky.

"And here you are causing all these problems in the hall. Trent, will you please put Marisa down? Trent, you go to practice. Marisa, I need to talk to you."

Marisa's heart dropped. The last thing she wanted to do was sit and talk to Mrs. Montgomery. She wasn't mean or anything, but she was the principal. "Let's go to my office," she suggested.

Marisa turned to Shane and Brandi. "I'll catch up with y'all when I'm done," she told them.

Once they were in the principal's office, Marisa became even more uncomfortable. Mrs. Montgomery took her seat at her gigantic desk and was looking down at Marisa. Marisa squirmed under the principal's gaze.

"Some of your teachers have voiced some concerns about your grades since your modeling jobs started. You are such a good student, Marisa. I would hate for you to fall too far behind."

"I'm trying, Mrs. Montgomery. I really am," she whined.

"I know, but I sat with you and your mom, and I agreed to let you take your work with you to Houston. She assured me that you were going to be able to handle working and school. Now here we are, nearly a month later, and some of your homework has been less than stellar. And you didn't do so well on your math midterm."

Marisa's head fell to her chest. "It's so hard to study when I'm in hair and makeup. I have to have a clear head when I shoot. I sleep on the way there and on the way back because I'm so tired. I don't know how to get it all done." She started to cry.

"It's okay. It's a brand new experience, but you have to adjust because if you don't, you will fail your classes."

Marisa had never made an F on her report card. She knew she had to pull it together. She thanked Mrs. Montgomery and left her office.

When she told Brandi and Shane her dilemma, they vowed to help. They had the same teachers and knew how important modeling was to Marisa's family right now. It wasn't like she could just give up on it. The Maldonados needed the money. They decided to head over to Jerry's to get Marisa caught up and eat some good burgers at the same time.

"Hey, I'm buying," she told them. "I'm cashing Gap checks now."

"Hook a sista up, then," Brandi told her.

"That's what I'm talking about. Free food courtesy of the Gap," Shane agreed.

They ate, they worked, and they laughed. "Good friends are so hard to find, and I found two," Marisa told her friends as they gathered their belongings. It had been a long day, but she did everything that she was supposed to do for work and school, and it just felt good.

CHAPTER 15

Brandi

*C*an I puleez come c u," Bryce texted. Normally, breaking up was hard for her, but this time it had been easy. Her father's presence back in her life had an impact on how she saw relationships. Her self-worth had returned. She was feeling like the Brandi from middle school who had just made cheerleader, who had just started dating Matthew Kincade—the best football player at Central Middle School.

If Bryce had sent that text to Brandi last year or even last semester, she would have probably given in. He didn't notice that she had changed. It happened so gradually, Brandi barely noticed it herself. But she *had* changed.

After a string of bad relationships, Brandi knew it was time to get strong. After Matthew cheated on her, she felt ruined. He started liking Marisa around the same time that she realized her father was falling further into his addiction. Then she met Brendon, who was a loser—on the football team and in life.

And then there was Camden, who turned out to be a stalker named Steven.

Now Bryce had to be added to the list of bad relationship choices. She knew one thing, she was never going to ignore red flags again or try to dismiss her internal early warning signs. She was done going down that road. No text was going to stop that.

Her father's recovery and presence was a huge part of her new outlook on her life and relationships. Whenever she thought of her dad now, she smiled, and her smiles felt genuine again. It hadn't been like that in a long time.

The night before, her father had taken her out on a date. It used to be a ritual with the two of them, but once his addiction got really bad, it was over. They were trying to get back to where they had once been.

He was working, and he wasn't wasting his money on drugs or stealing her mom's money. Their finances were better, so they had more money to enjoy each other. They could go out to eat more. They went shopping on Saturdays like they used to do. Life was good.

The doorbell startled Brandi out of her thoughts. Her father was at the door before she could make it down the stairs.

"Is Brandi home?" she heard Bryce's voice ask her father.

"Bran!" her father's voice was tense. "Bryce is here."

Hasn't he been paying attention? I'm done with this guy, she thought.

She stood at the top of the stairs. Her eyes told her father that she wasn't coming down. He turned back to Bryce. "I don't think Brandi wants to see you right now, Bryce. And frankly, I don't want to see you either. If you ever lay your hands on my daughter again, I will be after you faster than you—"

"Daddy!" Brandi hollered.

"Brandi!" Bryce yelled. "I'm sorry. I should never have blown up like that. You know I need you. Please don't do this."

"It's over, Bryce! Go home!" She wasn't budging.

"It's not over. I won't let you go! I can't!"

Her father grabbed Bryce by the neck and threw him against the door.

"Stop!" Brandi gasped, running down the stairs. She didn't want to be with Bryce, but she didn't want her dad to hurt him either.

"My daughter's done with you! You got that, kid!"

"Get yo' hands off me, old man, fo' I have to hurt you."

Brandi was trying to pry his fingers from Bryce's throat. "Stop it, Daddy."

"Don't let me catch you bothering my daughter again. You got that?"

By this time, Bryce was turning red. He could barely speak. His smart mouth was gone. "Yes, sir. I'll leave her alone."

Brandi watched as her father let him go. Bryce coughed, and tried to regain his composure and dignity. He turned and walked away. Brandi's father shut the door and faced his daughter.

Brandi had people on her side now. First Matthew had saved her from this creep and now her father. She knew that if there was a next time, she might not be so lucky. She knew that it was time for her to be alone. No more dating. No more boys.

"You have to be more careful in who

you choose to date, Bran," her father warned.

"You know what, Dad? I had a good time on our date last night. Maybe that's my kind of dating for right now."

James Haywood smiled. He knew that his sobriety was having a positive effect on his daughter, and he was pleased. "Sounds good to me," he said, hugging her. "Now go get Raven. I want to take you both out tonight."

"I'm right here," Raven said, eavesdropping from the stairs. They both laughed. It was classic Raven to be in everybody's business. "You know I have to make sure you're okay, B. You're my rock," she told her big sister, slipping on her flip-flops.

"Don't tell anybody, but you're mine too," she told her little sister. She picked Raven up and headed to the car.

Her father watched his two girls as he

locked up the house. *Thank God I'm home,* he thought. *Cat always had to work to keep us afloat. Well, I'm done with that. I need to man up. Thank God I'm home.*

CHAPTER 16

The Votes Are In

The Foster home was packed with guests for the election night party. It had already been a crazy day. Everyone had worked at the polls for twelve hours. Mrs. Foster and Mrs. Maldonado were at the house preparing to feed everyone.

Mr. Foster was happy that Clyde had agreed to return to the campaign. He had fired him in a fit of anger over the newspaper article that criticized his daughters.

Once he cooled off, he acknowledged that Clyde couldn't have stopped the article. He sincerely apologized and asked him to come back.

Brandi enlisted help from the cheer-leading squad. They were passing out stickers and pamphlets at supermarkets that detailed Mr. Foster's vision for the city. The twirlers had accompanied Marisa to polling locations across town, doing much of the same.

People wearing red, white, and blue *Foster for Fourteen* T-shirts swarmed the parking lots of both the public library and City Hall. Brian Foster was strategically working both locations while Clyde provided drinks and food for the workers.

"I'll be glad when this is over," Mr. Foster had admitted to his wife at noon when she stopped by to bring lunch for the campaign workers.

Mrs. Foster had many hats to wear throughout Election Day. First she had to alter larger-size T-shirts so they would attractively fit the tiny twirlers and cheerleaders. They had run out of extra-small shirts weeks ago. Luckily Shane and Robin were able to help their mom out.

On election morning, Mrs. Foster regretted not having Clyde order more T-shirts—in any size. When Shane told her there were twenty more girls who needed shirts, she ran to Walmart and purchased plain white Ts and iron-ons. There was a bit of trial and error, but finally, all of the girls had *Foster for Fourteen* across their shirts.

By the time everyone was in place, it was time to organize lunches. Then there was the dinner she would serve everyone once it was over. Mrs. Foster worked like a machine. Her nervous energy wouldn't let her sit for even a minute.

As she buzzed around Lupe Maldonado, waiting for their guests to arrive, Kim Foster was a ball of nerves. Mrs.

Maldonado gently touched her hand. "It's going to be okay. Brian has this."

"You just never know. Sometimes I wish he would have never agreed to do this. It's taken such a toll on the girls. Well, whatever happens, happens."

"Kim, your husband agreed to run for office to save my family. You know if George had never got into all that trouble in court, we wouldn't be having this conversation. Brian saved him. I know it's been tough for you all, and I'm sorry."

Kim turned to Lupe with tears in her eyes. It had been an emotional ride. "You don't ever have to be sorry. We would make the same decision if it happened again. There was no way that we could let George get deported, not after all he's done for this community. It wouldn't have been right."

"This is like a destiny thing, Kim. It was just supposed to be. This city needs

Brian. I'm telling you. It'll all be worth it in the end."

"What are you two in here babbling about?" Brian asked, walking through the door.

Kim wiped the tears from her face. "Did the polls close already?"

"They are closing. Are you okay?" he asked, concerned.

"Yes, baby," she said, kissing her husband gently. "It was just girl talk. Nothing for you to worry about."

The rest of the workers were close behind Mr. Foster. As they began to file into the house, one thing was for sure, they had worked up their appetites. Even though they had been at the polling stations all day, the ladies started to serve the hungry volunteers, who were watching the returns as they rolled in.

It wasn't looking good for the Foster campaign. The only numbers that had been calculated were those ballots that had been mailed. Stringer was in the lead, holding sixty-five percent of the vote.

Kim left the other ladies and joined her husband when the numbers came in for Port City. "This is nerve-wracking. If we don't win, I'm done with politics forever."

"Yeah, me too," he admitted. "This was more than I bargained for."

"Daddy, don't worry about the mail-in ballots," Shane said, listening to her parents' conversation. "I just know you have this."

One of the campaign workers chimed in, "You know Stringer padded those mail-in ballots. They've been doing it for years. The real numbers are coming soon."

The volunteer was right. The first polling location returns were reported. Everything changed. Mr. Foster was still behind with forty-seven percent of the vote, but he was closing in on his opponent.

Mrs. Foster began pouring a Texas-label sparkling wine for the final count.

"Come on, come on," Robin said impatiently.

Port City was one of the last cities because they were listed alphabetically. Everyone in the room was on the edge of their seats.

All of the surrounding cities had their final numbers, so they knew that Port City's numbers would be in too. And there it was, "Brian Foster, Area 14, 55% ..."

Everyone in the Foster house went wild. The teenagers were jumping up and down; they had been a part of something bigger than themselves. The adults were shaking Brian's hand and congratulating him. "You're just what this city needs," they told him.

Mrs. Foster cried, hugging Aiden. "We did it, little person," she said, kissing her grandchild.

Shane and Robin cried. It had been

physically and emotionally draining, but they did it.

Mr. Foster's phone vibrated in his pocket. It was Stringer. He congratulated him on a race well ran. His time representing Area 14 was over, but Mr. Foster knew that Stringer would always be there waiting for the next election. He was just that type.

After the numbers were revealed, the news reporters started giving comments about the winners. It was unanimous that the biggest upset was Area 14's, where the incumbent had lost to a first-time candidate. "Brian Foster's speech at City Hall probably put the nail in the coffin for Councilman Stringer," she said, playing a clip from that day. "Mr. Stringer was not available for comment."

Shane found her girls in the sea of people that crowded into their downstairs. "Hey, come upstairs with me," she told them. When they got to her room, she turned to them with tears in her eyes. "Thank you for everything. I couldn't have made it through this without you."

"You know we'll always have your back," Brandi told her.

Marisa shook her head in agreement. "I'm just glad that he won. All of his hard work paid off."

"So you think Mrs. Smith will let you turn all your science assignments in late now that you're dad's a council member?" Brandi teased.

"Yeah, and maybe you'll get a reserved table at Jerry's since you're famous now," Marisa said, joining in on the fun. "Maybe Robin'll get her own parking space!"

Shane smiled and shook her head at her two friends.

Project Graduation

I can't get you into Project Graduation," Shane told Marisa and Brandi. They begged to assist her with the photography she had been assigned to do for the senior class. The senior class party was strictly off limits to anyone without an invitation.

"But this is Trent's last day as a Port City High Wildcat, and I have to spend it with him. You have to need help with *something*," Marisa whined.

"And I just wanna go," Brandi told her. "I'm bored."

"You two are impossible. The seniors don't want to celebrate with underclassmen. That will ruin the night for them."

"We could wear disguises," Brandi said, picking up the Mardi Gras mask that they had worn in the parade.

"Oh, I like that idea," Marisa told them. "Disguises!"

"Y'all dumb. That's a horrible idea, but let me call Mrs. Monroe and see what I can do." Shane made a call and detailed all of the equipment and shots that she needed to take for the senior class. She explained to Mrs. Monroe how difficult her job was going to be, and she requested two assistants. Mrs. Monroe told her to give the other team members a call and see if they could help her.

"It seems that everyone is gone already for some trip or other. I've tried calling several people from our team. Is it possible that Marisa and Brandi could help me? They've worked with me a lot before on personal shoots, so they know what needs to be done. They'll be really helpful, I promise."

"That's a wonderful idea, Shane. I'll just let Mrs. Montgomery know that they'll be accompanying you. Have fun and work hard."

"Thanks, Mrs. Monroe."

Marisa and Brandi were as eager as five-year-olds on Halloween. As soon as she hung up the phone, they pounced on her. "We knew you could come up with something!" Brandi told her.

"You are my girl, for real!" shouted Marisa.

"Yeah, yeah, yeah, y'all get dressed 'cause you are helping me for real. Put on all black too. Don't even try to be all fancy. We are there to work."

"Yes, ma'am," Brandi said smartly.

"I'll call my mom right now to bring my clothes."

"Me too," Marisa told her.

By the time they left, they looked artistic and hip. "I could get used to this look," Brandi told Shane, looking in the mirror seductively. "Let me see your camera."

"No, you're too clumsy. Besides, we've gotta get going. My mom is getting antsy. She's gonna pick us up too, so she wants to get a little sleep."

In the car, Shane ran down their job duties. "B, you can take care of the lighting; Marisa, you can be in charge of positioning people for their pictures. They don't even hire a photographer anymore now that I'm getting my professional on. Plus, I'm free."

They set up for pictures, but they didn't open the booth for another hour. They wanted to get the seniors in action as they indulged in the festivities. There were carnival games with prizes, tables set up for dominoes and card games like gin rummy and hearts, raffles, and food.

The movie was scheduled to play at midnight, and the seniors would be served popcorn and refreshments. Pizza Inn sponsored the event. There was a buffet set up in the cafeteria. Marisa was hard at work when Trent, Ashton, and Dalton arrived. She was helping Shane with shots of students getting pizza and salads from the buffet area.

"What are you doing here?" Trent asked, surprised. They had seen each other at his graduation earlier that day, but she never told him that she was coming tonight.

"I wanted to spend your last night of high school with you, so I'm helping Shane with photography," Marisa said with a sly smile.

"Hey, my future baby mama is here,

everybody, so don't try to get fresh with me tonight," Ashton said, hugging Shane and kissing her on the cheek.

"Boy, move. I'm working. I don't have time to play, Ash."

"Girl, you make time. I'm leaving for the army this summer. You are going to miss me."

"Let me get through the night, and I'll worry about missing you tomorrow."

"You are mean, Shane Foster."

"And you love it," she said, getting back to her work. *Last day of Ashton,* she thought. *You know I hate to say it, but I think I just might miss that fool.*

"And what about me?" Ryan asked. Shane turned around quickly when she heard Ryan's voice.

Shane didn't know what to say. Somewhere inside, she regretted not taking their relationship further. She knew it was a mistake, but she also knew that she would be more hurt saying good-bye. He wasn't the type to stay in Port City. She knew if it was supposed to happen, they would meet again.

"Yeah," she finally said, "I'm going to miss you." Her voice was serious, and he reached out to hold her in his arms.

When he let her go, he went back into boss mode and said, "You're slacking off. Is this what I taught you?"

Shane went back to taking pictures.

The seniors were going to be released after they were served breakfast at six a.m. But Shane, Marisa, and Brandi left at two, after they'd fulfilled their duties.

"Waffle House?" Shane asked them. "My mom said she'd take us. I'm starving and a little depressed."

"Me too," Marisa said, looking out of the window. "There will never be another Trent Walker at Port City High. He was one of a kind. I can't believe he's leaving."

"Arkansas isn't that far away," Brandi said, trying to cheer up her friend.

"Yeah, B. It *is* that far away," Marisa said. She lost it and started crying. "Who am I without him?"

"A friend, a sister, a twirler, an actress, and a model," Shane said, listing Marisa's many accomplishments. "I can't lie. I'm going to miss them too, Ashton and Ryan." That broke the tension in the car. At the same time, they all started laughing.

"Yeah, it has less punch when there's two of them," Brandi told her.

"I know, but it's so hard to choose just one, and now there's none. We're going to be all alone next year." They pulled into the parking lot at Waffle House. "But if we have to be alone, I'm just glad that we'll be alone together."

"Yeah, me too." A small smile appeared on Brandi's face. "Bright side—we are the new junior class."

"Riiight, I hadn't even thought about it. We are upperclassmen now," Marisa said, looking at her friends.

"Ride or die?" Shane asked.

"Ride or die," Brandi and Marisa said together.

ABOUT THE AUTHOR

Shannon Freeman

$\mathcal{B}$orn and raised in Port Arthur, Texas, Shannon Freeman works full time as an English teacher in her hometown. After completing college at Oral Roberts University, Freeman began her work in the classroom teaching English and oral communications. At that time, the characters of her breakout series, Port City High, began to form, but these characters would not come to life for years. An apartment fire destroyed almost all of the young teacher's worldly possessions before she could begin writing. With nothing to lose, Freeman packed up and headed to Los Angeles, California, to pursue a passion that burned within her since her youth, the entertainment industry.

Beginning in 2001, Freeman made numerous television appearances and enjoyed a rich life full of friends and hard work. In 2008, her world once again changed when she and her husband, Derrick Freeman, found out that they were expecting their first child. Freeman then made the difficult decision to return to Port Arthur and start the family that she had always wanted.

At that time, Freeman returned to the classroom, but entertaining others was still a desire that could not be quenched. Being in the classroom again inspired her to tell the story of Marisa, Shane, and

Brandi that had been evolving for almost a decade. She began to write and the Port City High series was born.

Port City High is the culmination of Freeman's life experiences, including her travels across the United States and Europe. Her stories reflect the friendships she's made across the globe. Port City High is the next breakout series for today's young adult readers. Freeman says, "The topics are relevant and life changing. I just hope that people are touched by my characters' stories as much as I am."